JESSE CROSSE

A NOVEL

"What would happen if the Messiah appeared as a black teenager on a high school basketball team in a small Southern town? Michael J. Moran's always interesting and sometimes provocative novel will evoke new ideas and interesting discussions for both younger and older readers. Clever allusions to characters, places, and events from the Gospel narratives are nothing less than brilliant."

—**JOHN M. KEITH,** Episcopal priest and author of
  True Divinity in Christ: a Testimony of Faith & Hope

MICHAEL J. MORAN
JESSE CROSSE
A NOVEL

Parkhurst Brothers, Inc., Publishers

LITTLE ROCK

www.pbros.net

Parkhurst Brothers books are distributed to the trade through the Chicago Distribution Center, a unit of the University of Chicago Press, and may be ordered through Ingram Book Company, Baker & Taylor, Follett Library Resources and other book industry wholesalers. To order from the University of Chicago's Chicago Distribution Center, phone 1-800-621-2736 or send a fax to 1-800-621-8476. Copies of this and other Parkhurst Brothers, Inc., Publishers titles are available to organizations and corporations for purchase in quantity by contacting Special Sales Department at our home office location, listed on our website. Manuscript submission guidelines for this publishing company are available at our website.

Manufactured in the United States of America

First Edition 2011

2011 2012 2013 2014 2015 2016 2017 2018   16 15 14 13 12 11 10 9 8 7 6 5 4 3 2 1

Library of Congress Control Number: 2009942593

ISBN: Trade Paperback: 978-1-935166-44-3   [10-digit: 1-935166-44-1] $10.00

An e-book edition of this title is available.

Design Director and Dust-jacket/cover design:
Wendell E. Hall

Page design:
Shelly Culbertson

Acquired for Parkhurst Brothers, Inc., Publishers by:
Ted Parkhurst

Editor:
Roger Armbrust

Proofreader:
Barbara Paddack

To Roger Armbrust

and Ted Parkhurst,

without whom Jesse would

never have come to life.

CHAPTER ONE

For the first time in 50 years I was driving on Highway 21, a sun-baked strip of asphalt with too many potholes. At a spot in the road with ancient, lofty pines on both sides, I pulled off onto the shoulder, got out of my car, and walked a few steps into knee-high bushes where I thought I remembered the roadside sign had once stood. I found the two wooden posts that had held it upright, both still showing the marks of the axe that had caused the sign to fall. The turmoil of that time five decades ago at first led no one to notice the fallen sign. Other events overwhelmed it.

The sign went up on a Monday, and the attack on it took place that night. The vandal was never discovered. It would, in normal times, have been of urgent importance. But the events of that night paralyzed ordinary thought and action. The mayor eventually sent two local men to drag the sign from the woods, load it on a pickup truck, and dispose of it. It was never replaced. I guess the pain associated with its fall was too great to confront. Then, perhaps, the desire to forget overcame the impulse to remember. Two stumps provided the only evidence that the sign ever existed.

Even though a large number of people vital to this story have moved away, as I did, I thought it worthwhile to come back and see if the sign and the memories had returned. Did people in my hometown still recall the story? The passage of half a century wipes away many images—especially the things people would rather forget. Perhaps I was too close to the story and think it's more important than it really is. But I returned to Jewelton, where I lived for the first 18 years of my life, to revive my own memories, and to make sure, before the death of the last one of us who remembers, that people of Jewelton hear the story of Jesse Crosse.

Though my part in the story is minor, I should identify myself. I'm Luke Anteock, a 69-year-old doctor who has been in general practice my entire working career at least half a continent away from my home town. For all practical purposes I haven't lived in Jewelton since I was 18. Back in September of 1960 I was beginning my senior year in high school and expecting it to be a great experience. I was so positive that the year would be worth remembering that I kept a detailed journal of its events—a girl would probably have called it a *diary*—but I was more comfortable with the word *journal*. I re-read all of it before making the trip home, wanting the details to be clear in my mind.

At the outset of my last year in high school I was sure that I would be going to college, and I had vague hopes of becoming a doctor. It may sound odd, but it was because of my long stint as manager of the basketball team that thoughts of a medical career first entered my mind. Just taping ankles and applying balm to sore muscles suggested to me that maybe this was the first step to becoming a physician. Plus, the guys on the team and even the coach called me "Doc." I'm a little embarrassed now to admit that the source of my career inspiration was nothing more than that.

I don't claim anything special about the beauty of Jewelton as 1960's summer began to shift to fall. I've seen the same colorful effects in many places. In many ways it looked like a lot of other small towns in the South. I know, because I saw more than a few of them travelling to basketball games. Jewelton had its Main Street, with its Woolworth's and a Rexall Drug and a Piggly Wiggly—a grocery chain located throughout southern states in those days. What business there was in Jewelton was located on Main, too—including my dad's law office. The wide concrete expanse of our main thoroughfare made angled parking possible and gave the street a leisurely look. None of that big-city parallel parking for us. The town had a little over 2,000 people then, though I understand it's only about half that now. Jewelton High School had been built during the Depression by the W.P.A. Its exterior was local stone and mortar—not especially attractive, but it looked sturdy. The elementary school was built the same, located a couple of blocks away from the high school; each was three blocks off Main.

My school, the smallest in our county, was set to guide its 34 oldest students through their final preparations for the future. I was almost vibrating with anticipation. A student beginning the senior year of high school is likely to be an optimist about most things. The accomplishments of the previous senior class look vulnerable to those who have inherited their position. They see themselves as being capable of doing more than their predecessors. The Senior Prom would be superior in its decorations, music, and the quality and quantity of food served. The school play would be funnier or more dramatic, since the acting would be dominated by this year's seniors rather than last year's. Our grades would be better, our leaders more effective, our senior project more lasting in its effect on the school. We were enthusiastic about every category of student life except one—athletics.

Actually, "athletics" at Jewelton amounted to basketball only. The size of our school, coupled with the limitations of the school board's budget, eliminated our participating in any other sport. It was only in basketball that we seniors weren't going to make much of a mark. Our team in the previous year had won only nine games and lost 22. And all the players who started for that team had graduated, leaving replacements of doubtful quality. Our class was energetic, smart, and blessed with leadership, but we didn't have anybody who could consistently hit a jump shot.

Maybe I'm exaggerating what I thought in September 1960 about the shortcomings of our team, but we really had little more than barely competent players to take over the starting positions. I knew, because I was not only the trainer and manager, but, other than Coach Mo Levitson, I was the unofficial, self-appointed assistant talent estimator. Neither one of us was optimistic about the coming season.

As Coach Levitson and I cleaned up the equipment room in early September, he said, "Luke, a coach is always supposed to be looking on the bright side of things to keep up morale, but I can't for the life of me figure how we're going to win even nine games this year."

My relationship with Coach Levitson had developed to a point that, after administering to him and his players for three years, I felt almost as if I were his assistant coach rather than just the manager. He was probably in his mid-50s, stocky but still trim and energetic. His curly white hair was the object of much abuse when, sitting on the sidelines during games, he had to witness multiple examples of his team's pitiful attempts to play basketball. Seeing them, he'd run his right hand through his hair from front to back so roughly that I wondered why he wasn't balding. And yet, on those far-too-many occasions of bad play, the most potent exclamation of disappointment that I ever heard him say was "Dad-gum-it!" He was a prince of a man, and I felt lucky to have been his manager since I was a ninth-grader.

When, as he rarely did, he would mention his fears and doubts about a team, I knew he depended on me to keep my mouth shut. And I did. In the case of the '60-'61 team, he could see, with an eye trained during three decades of coaching, that Jewelton was facing a tough season.

"Coach, we've got a couple of pretty good guys; we just don't have one really good guy."

Like many of the coaching profession, Coach Levitson addressed me and the players in a paternal manner, using the word *son* in a way that we never questioned. It was as if we took it for granted that some vague but real family relationship existed between us when we worked together under the auspices of sport. It was as if *Son* had become a proper noun—in the same way that *Coach* had.

"Son, if we had a six-foot-eight center who averaged 25 points and 15 rebounds a game, which we obviously don't, I still don't see how we could finish in the top three. Our league is loaded this year. Now if that big fellow had a twin brother who was just as good as he was, we might have something." I agreed that it would take more than one excellent player to make Jewelton a contender for the league championship. Our players were just too ordinary.

On another day when I was at the gym, checking the condition of the game jerseys and shorts, I wondered for the umpteenth time why everything about Jewelton's basketball program was so wrong. I looked forlornly at our team's name printed on the front of each jersey. I questioned whether any team had a nickname so poorly chosen to indicate athletic skill or something to be feared. We weren't known as "Cougars" or "Demons" or "Warriors"— we were stuck with the sorry description as "Anglers." Fishermen, for Pete's sake! Just because a lot of Jewelton business, the tourist trade, was connected with Lake Tiberias and its plentiful supply of bass and bream, did that mean we had to be advertisers of the town's commercial interests? Have you ever heard of another team with that name? We did get mentioned once in a short *Sports Illustrated* article about odd team names, but that didn't make me feel any better about it.

I couldn't count the number of times that name caused our teams to endure put-downs and insults. It was rare that we ever traveled to another gym without seeing lots of signs from our "hosts" proclaiming that "Something smells fishy!" or "Welcome, Fishing League Champions." We were the butt of all the jokes.

I thought Coach Levitson was part of the problem. He was a great guy, no doubt about that, but I couldn't believe that he was the type of coach Jewelton needed to be a real winner. He was just too old-fashioned, unable to compete with the league's younger coaches. He'd been at our school for his entire career, and I didn't believe that coaching was his main concern.

He taught three classes a day, and I knew of no other coach who did that, except for those who watched over P.E. classes. And Coach Levitson taught English! He even required his students to address him as "Mister" rather than "Coach" if we were talking to him either in or about English class.

He was an excellent teacher—knowledgeable, demanding, and fair. And if anybody thought basketball players were going to get a free ride in his classes, that person was altogether wrong. I can testify that things were just the opposite. He expected his players (and manager!) to set the curve in his classes, whether we were juniors in American Literature or seniors in British Literature. He never allowed anyone associated with the team to excuse himself from handing in assignments or missing a test because we got home late from a road game.

With Coach Levitson at the wheel of our team bus, and driving at his customary 50 miles an hour, it wasn't unusual to get back to school near midnight when we had a long trip home from a place like Cemaria. Once, when I was a sophomore, I was as amazed as anyone to hear that Coach had given Paul Lightman—our best player—a zero on a test. It was because Paul hadn't been at school the day after a Thursday out-of-town game during which he had sprained an ankle. But Paul had shown up for that night's Friday dance in the gym, though he didn't dance. The fact that he was there was enough for Coach Levitson.

He informed Paul the following Monday that he had flunked the test. That took place just before the Christmas holidays, and when report cards came out in early January, the news that Paul had flunked British Literature burned up Jewelton's telephone lines. Paul's "F" meant he was dropped from the team for the rest of the season. Coach Levitson's decision to give Paul the zero was widely blamed for what followed.

Our team died a nasty death, and I could tell that Coach was suffering the most. His grim demeanor for the rest of the schedule was unmistakable for its cause. Worst of all, he really liked Paul, who was as good a guy as he was a player. But Paul had violated Coach's rules—"Ten Points for Players"—that all on the team were expected to follow to the letter. Vital to the Ten Points was this stipulation: No player should take for himself any privilege that other, non-playing students didn't have as well. Coach judged that Paul had violated that rule when he absented himself from the test but came to the dance.

It was Coach's insistence on these rules and his enthusiasm for teaching literature that made me think he wasn't committed enough to basketball. He couldn't bring the Anglers to a respected position in our league. We never heard of students, especially players, at other schools, having to toe the line as rigidly as did Mo Levitson's players.

When I would see him in his office before a game, reading Thomas Hardy or Nathaniel Hawthorne, it never seemed right. If he wanted to read, how about something from Hank Iba or Adolph Rupp? Those great college coaches could teach him something about basketball better than a 19th century novelist could.

I knew that Coach Levitson had a special place in his heart for his players. He treated them with respect, good humor, and care. But he was determined that they should be the exemplars of what a Jewelton student should be; it was hard to live up to his standards. I thought they placed a burden on any boy who wanted to play basketball for the Anglers. Anyway, having checked out the condition of the jerseys with the absurd name, I stacked them back on the shelves. I then turned to pumping up basketballs, which were also in the equipment room next to Coach's office. He came in, settled into the folding metal chair at his desk, and pulled his *British Voices* textbook from his brief case.

Looking in to the room where I was working, he said, "Finished your homework yet, Doc?" With the pump still in my hand, I stepped into his office to respond.

"Not yet, Coach."

"*Mister* Levitson, Doc."

"Sorry. No, Mr. Levitson, not yet."

"You'll like *Beowulf* best when the protagonist meets up with Grendel. Now, you'll probably be initially attracted by lines like (and here he recited from memory), 'The crimson currents bubbled and heaved and…reddened with gore,' but you're bright enough to see beyond that surface appeal to an appreciation of the courage that it takes for Beowulf to tackle the job—in a fight that isn't even his."

I basked in his compliment—that I could go beyond the ordinary in my analysis of the epic—but I wasn't sure I deserved it. I knew that if I was looking forward to anything in reading the ancient story, it was the bloody battle between hero and monster. I reminded myself to try to see even more.

"Mr. Levitson," I wondered, "how many times have you read *Beowulf*?"

"I'm not certain, Doc. I suppose 30 times or so."

"Do you still like reading it?"

"Doc, it's like most works that endure in literature. There's more to it than meets the eye, and you discover that the second, third, or 30th time you read it. Even if it's a nursery rhyme—if it lasts, there's depth to it, or a point of view we don't get tired of hearing or being reminded about. So I anticipate enjoying the reading assignment for the 31st time, yes."

"So you haven't done the homework either?" I smilingly observed.

He grinned back and confidently declared, "No, but I'll have it finished by class tomorrow!"

Encouraged by the nature of the conversation, I pushed a bit into the area about Coach Levitson that I never understood. I wasn't sure exactly how to proceed, but I wanted to know more. I left caution behind:

"Mr. Levitson isn't it kind of unusual for somebody to coach basketball and teach literature, too? I mean, I've never heard of that combination before."

He smiled as my last words tumbled down on him sitting there. I was switching the pump quickly from one hand to the other, a bit nervous about the intrusive nature of my question. As he lifted his head to speak, he looked like a man addressing the heavens about his role in life. "You're absolutely right, Son. Not too many folks have that combination. Most people seem to think I'm odd for it, but to me it has always made good sense. Since you never had the opportunity to take Latin here at Jewelton High, I'll translate the words I'm about to use: *Mens sana in corpore sano,* 'A sound mind in a sound body.' It's an ancient ideal of man's perfect combination. He would be a man of intelligence who is also capable of action. That's not the stereotype of an intellectual who can't throw a ball 60 feet, or of the athlete who can't spell his own name. It's the best of both worlds. For 30 years I've tried to encourage that in our boys, and the girls, too. I just can't see developing one without the other. So, I've tried to demonstrate that in my own life. The students know I'm fond of books, but they also know I can still run laps with the team and take part in basketball practice when we're a man short. Does that make sense to you?"

It did. Although I was noted for getting about the best grades in our class, at least among the boys, I was always conscious of and regretful about my athletic inability. I would have liked to have been one of those "ideal" types of men, whose soundness of body matched the powers of his mind. And I could, come to think of it, think of no adult other than Coach Levitson who had as good a combination of the two skills.

"Speaking of my taking part in practice," the coach interjected, "I'm afraid that despite my words about the sound body, that I'm getting too old to do it much longer, and we may have to suit you up if we don't get a few more out for the team this year."

The problem that he referred to only compounded our basketball woes. Only nine boys had indicated an interest in playing this year. We couldn't even practice properly with that number. The thought that I might have to be thrown into the practice sessions was a good barometer that we were in deep trouble. Somebody would have to fill in the gap. But who?

CHAPTER TWO

Since I imagined myself as something more than just the Anglers' manager, I took it upon myself to solve Coach Levitson's latest problem: lack of players. My motive was more than a little selfish. I really had no urge to become directly involved in the team's scrimmages at practice. I've already referred to my lack of sports talent. And although coach's "ideal" of sound mind-sound body was attractive, I had no compelling desire to try to achieve that worthy goal at what seemed like such a late stage of my life.

I was content to busy myself with managerial and training duties at practice. That ordinarily meant that after the players had gone to the gym from the locker room, and I had picked up towels and stray pieces of tape and whatever else was left lying about, I had time for doing my homework or reading. I liked the environment of the dressing room under those circumstances. It felt insulated and remote from the muffled whistles and shoe squeaks and occasional yells coming from the gym. When Coach Levitson needed me, which was only rarely, he bellowed "Anteock!" in a certain tone that after three years I invariably could distinguish from all the other noises emanating from practice sessions. I had grown too fond of this role to relinquish it for a more involved one. I knew and liked my place. So I was eager to help both the team and myself by finding some more players, or at least willing bodies, to fill out our squad.

Although I mentioned before that I considered myself a judge of basketball talent, I have to admit that my ability was limited to players who were already team members. I had never been in the business of being a talent scout, trying to round up new players. My forte was making critical evaluations of boys already going through Coach Levitson's drills and attempting to carry out his instructions, not determining who might be able to do these things. We had 15 boys in the senior class, and five of these were presently team members. No one of the remaining 10 (including me) even remotely qualified as a possibility. They, like me, had neither the inclination nor the talent to stand as substitutes for the Anglers. The search would have to be among the underclassmen.

Right after I finished with my chores in the equipment room and the talk with Coach Levitson, I was determined to begin the hunt. I had no authority to hold try-outs for newcomers—as a matter of fact, the Coach had previously held a tryout open to all. That is how we knew that only nine students were interested in being Anglers. What I needed was information—information about who hadn't turned out for the original muster of players, but who could and would join up at this late date.

As I walked out of the ancient Jewelton gym, locking the door behind me, I thought of John Mercer. Not that Mercer was in any way a possibility to add to the team's numbers, but that he might be the one to know who could. Mercer, a senior, had the reputation for being an oddball. Blade-thin with a burr haircut and no apparent interest in his clothes or how he looked, he was probably the smartest kid in our class, but he never seemed to be concerned about making his mark in the classroom. He always had other fish to fry— couldn't be bothered with the usual avenues of high school achievement. He was a loner who lived farther away from Jewelton than any other student I knew of, way out in the woods. Reading about Henry David Thoreau when I was a junior, I thought immediately of Mercer. His distance from school was matched by his distance from other people. Loaded with opinions about almost everything, he was not reluctant to let them be known. I remember well one of the famous Mercer comments in class: One day in Civics he suggested and defended furiously and quite effectively the notion that what the United States needed was a King. None of the students actually argued with him about it, but Mrs. Jackson, the teacher, was probably compelled to dispute the matter. She was the official upholder of the American Way in that class. The rest of us stayed out of it because Mercer was already known to be a very prickly customer, and very sharp and well read to boot.

Mrs. Jackson did her best, but Mercer wasn't discouraged by her objections. I can't recall many of the details of their exchange, except that Mercer was quoting names of politicians and titles of books all over the place, and although the rest of us had no idea who any of his sources were, we were much impressed by his jousting ability. There was some degree of satisfaction on our part that one of us could so effectively tangle with a teacher. Perhaps it was mean of us, but we enjoyed and took pride in his skill at making Mrs. Jackson squirm. I also recall that Mercer himself took no satisfaction from the debate. After class, quite a few of us approached the usually unapproachable

Mercer to say, "You really got her!" and he turned on us and said something to the effect that he wasn't interested in making Mrs. Jackson look bad, he just wanted to argue his point.

Another unusual thing about Mercer was that he took on a task that hardly seemed to fit in with his other interests. Since he was a sophomore he had been the sports editor of the school newspaper. It always struck me as strange that someone whose mind was busy with things that most of his peers hadn't even heard of would devote time to something as ordinary as athletics.

But Mercer knew sports well. His columns were never dull. If there was any one theme to his writing, it was that Coach Levitson was too advanced in his approach to basketball for most Jewelton students and townspeople to appreciate. If that sort of writing had come from anyone other than Mercer, the suspicions would have been thick that it was just a matter of a student trying to get into the good graces of the coach. But no one ever suspected that of Mercer. He never hung around Coach Levitson and was no more or less argumentative with him than he was with any other teacher. In class with Mr. Levitson, Mercer often disagreed with him about the meaning and value of poems, short stories, and practically everything else we read. Mr. Levitson was almost sure to turn in Mercer's direction after delivering an opinion or interpretation, ready to field an objection or contrary view from Mercer. I could tell that Mercer got on Mr. Levitson's nerves from time to time, but he always heard him out, and sometimes even agreed with him!

It appeared to me that all the other faculty members had taken a vow to do two things with regard to Mercer: refrain from wringing his neck no matter how much they might like to do it, and never agree with him. Only Mr. Levitson would ever credit Mercer with having valid points. Even though Mercer was one of Coach's biggest defenders, we knew that had nothing to do with Mr. Levitson's treatment of Mercer in class. The role of Mr. and Coach were too firmly separated in Levitson's mind to allow one to influence the other. Could and would Mercer help me? I had nothing more than a slight hope, but I decided to act on it before I changed my mind.

Leaving the gym behind, I guessed that Mercer would still be in the tiny room which housed *The Hook*, which, of course, was the name of our newspaper. I re-entered the school and made the long walk to the end of the hall where I hoped to find him still at work. He was there, and alone, although he wasn't working on his column. Seeing the numbers and letters written on its spine, I could tell he was reading a library book, one so bulky and ancient that I wondered why Mrs. Finley, our librarian, would stock such a volume for teenagers. But Mercer wasn't a typical teenager.

He glanced at me only briefly as I entered, and I got the immediate impression that he wasn't happy to be interrupted while reading. I wasn't discouraged by his reception, because I didn't expect a warm welcome.

"Mercer, I'm glad you're still here, I was looking for you."

He seemed somewhat surprised by that and responded only with a quizzical look that seemed to say, "Explain yourself."

"I'm trying to find some new blood for the Anglers, and I thought I might get some ideas from you."

Mercer put his book down slowly and glanced around the office as if he were trying to locate the person I had asked for help. When he finally decided that I was indeed addressing him, he motioned me to sit down. To this point he had uttered not a word, this usually talkative fellow; so I plunged ahead.

"You know we've got a problem with numbers. We've only got nine guys and we can't even practice with that. Do you have any idea of who else we could get?"

Finally, a response, as he blurted with a laugh, "What's the matter, Anteock, is Levitson threatening to draft you onto the team?" He had an uncanny way of going to the heart of things, especially when a person would like to keep something less-than-obvious.

"I suppose you could say that is one of my concerns." I responded. "But there's more to it than that." I quickly adopted his manner of referring to Coach as I continued, "Levitson is getting too old to fill-in for teenagers at practice. I'm afraid he might drop over any day now. Besides, when he's practicing with the team he can't see everything that's going on." My expressed concern about Coach's well being was exaggerated, but it seemed a valid point.

Mercer's reply was in keeping with his printed views of the basketball dilemma at Jewelton: "He can't coach properly because his players are too stupid to figure out what he's trying to get them to do."

I had no desire to discuss Mercer's analysis of how Coach was trying to install a system that his players never understood and the average fan didn't appreciate. But Mercer wasn't through: "Anteock, you above all people should be able to see the man's system by now. You've spent more time at practice than anybody who isn't a player. You can see what it's all about, can't you?" What Mercer didn't know is how little time I actually spent viewing practice, huddled up in my dressing-room cocoon with my books.

"Well, sure," I lamely responded, "I suppose I know what he's doing as well as anyone."

"Then you know that what the fans in this town want in our team is totally at odds with Levitson's philosophy."

I knew no such thing. And I wished I had read Mercer's *Hook* columns more carefully so I could discuss Levitson's "philosophy" with him. I didn't know what he was driving at, so I bluffed my way past his point.

"We know what Coach wants," I said, "but how can he get there without more players? The team's in trouble. Who do you think can we get to help the team?" I thought that if I made it sound as if he alone could solve the problem he might have a suggestion. A guy with an eye as sharp as his might have seen someone the rest of us had missed.

He didn't rise to the bait. Instead of a suggestion he had another question: "Anteock, tell me your description of the one player who could lift the Jewelton basketball team to respectability. What would he be like?"

An easy question. "He'd be 6-10—could jump through the roof, average 38 points a game and 20 rebounds—and help me clean up the locker room after the game." That was just the right mix of basketball savvy and humor, I thought.

"You left out something vital," he snapped.

"What else? A beautiful sister who loves managers?" My wit was on parade.

Mercer wasn't amused. He leaned forward in his chair and stared hard at me, an uncomfortable moment. The look was one I'd seen before: the one he had just prior to boring into a teacher who had said something upon which Mercer was about to pounce. Even though he was a short, skinny kid, he could be intellectually lethal. He reminded me of a mongoose about to make his lightning-quick strike.

"One little detail you left out, Anteock—what was the color of this savior of Jewelton?"

I immediately knew what he meant. The common talk around town was that the main reason Jewelton was falling even further behind other towns was that we had no supply of "colored" players to draw on—a sight becoming common on the other teams in our league. The recent influx of Negro players in newly integrated schools had given them a high profile and rescued them from the obscurity of the segregated leagues they had played in before. As consolidation of schools began to undo the inequality of "separate but equal" schools throughout the country, athletes who had starred in tiny venues were now getting to make a bigger splash, showing their skills to many who had never before seen them.

But Jewelton was in a county of so few Negroes that segregated schools hadn't even existed. The miniscule number of Negro children had always attended Jewelton's schools. Typically the number of Negroes in grades one through twelve was not much more than a handful. That was probably true on the day that Mercer and I talked, and from that tiny group no great athletes had ever emerged to change Jewelton's basketball history. Mercer continued to stare at me, waiting for my reply.

"I see what you're getting at, but I don't think the guy would have to be a Negro," I finally said. That was my belief, though I have since wondered if in the back of my mind I didn't dream of a tall, rampaging, and, yes, black star who would lead the Anglers to victory after victory.

Mercer paused and then dissected my words: "I notice you didn't use any of the typical, hostile racial references when describing him. You are to be commended, Anteock."

I wasn't sure if he was sincere or sarcastic. Mercer wasn't easy to figure. His sly smile made me realize that he was still two steps ahead of me, and I had no idea what was coming next.

"How serious is Levitson about adding to the team? Do you think he'd consider some guys who haven't ever played any organized ball?"

I wasn't authorized to speak for Coach, but I knew that he'd be relieved if he could put at least two fives on the floor for the sake of normal practice—plus a couple more if possible, since we were scheduled to play a junior varsity game before every varsity contest. A dozen players would solve a couple of serious problems.

"Mercer, if you know any other ballplayers, I think you owe it to the basketball program you have so faithfully followed in your *Hook* columns. This is your school, too, you know. Do you actually have anybody in mind, or are you just getting your mental gymnastics exercises at my expense?" I was irritated by what felt like a cat-and-mouse game he might be playing. Maybe I asked for it by coming to him for advice, but I wasn't going to put up with it much longer. "Do you know anybody or not?"

He could tell I was on the verge of leaving. I thought I detected a note of conciliation as he leaned back in his chair and surprisingly said, "I may have exactly what the team needs."

CHAPTER THREE

September of 1960 was drawing to a close. Summer's heat was loosening its stranglehold, and the cool mornings signaled the teachers that they could turn off the classroom fans. This meant I had little time to find a solution to our manpower problem. I had talked to Mercer two days before, and he had promised to look into the matter. I had concluded that he was bragging about having "exactly" what our team needed. Maybe that day he just didn't want to admit he couldn't help us, despite his alleged authority about what ailed the Jewelton basketball team. My own thinking had turned up no one who could qualify as an extra hand. Though I didn't know every kid in our school, I supposed that, since opening day, I had seen them all, including the ninth-graders who were new to the school. Nobody stood out.

I was just arriving to school that morning when I saw Mercer making a bee-line down the hall. He was walking at an accelerated pace. His slender frame sliced the air. But this was his usual means of locomotion—always going as if great matters were at hand that needed his immediate attention. I expected him to buzz right past me, but he stopped abruptly and gave me one of those eyeball-to-eyeball stares.

"It's all set, Anteock," he blurted. "I've got your players. Of course, you'll need converting, like everyone else—except Levitson. But you'll see the light. You'll become a believer." His intensity was palpable. His enthusiasm was almost catching, but I was sure that whatever had generated his ardor would be hard for me to swallow.

"Mercer, when you start by talking about the need to 'convert' me, I'm suspicious. Who have you dug up? You're not the only person I've talked to about this, and everybody else says there are no players to be found."

He flashed a knowing grin, implying that I was a poor soul unable to see the light. His know-it-all attitude was irritating. I knew I had played upon his vanity when I tried to enlist his help, but now it was just annoying. Despite what he must have seen in my reaction, he confidently told me in an undertone, as if we were co-conspirators of a sort, "You asked me to find players. OK, I found four. And they aren't just practice fill-ins and B-teamers! One of them is going to be great! The other guys will work out OK because they complement him. They can play his brand of ball, which, by the way, Mo Levitson has been trying to preach all these years. Don't judge these guys rashly. They are keepers!"

As we were standing in front of my locker, I began to twirl the dial idly, making it clear to Mercer that I didn't consider his news very important. I knew he was capable of wild imaginative flights, and his latest revelation only served to make me think he'd lost touch with reality. Four players? And one of them "great"? Suddenly a thought occurred to me. Maybe he was on to something!

"Mercer, is this 'great' player a transfer? Did he just move in over the weekend?" Perhaps he had mined an area I had overlooked.

"He didn't just move to town. He's been here since school opened; he came from the memorably named town of Flower. He moved in over the summer. He's a sophomore."

"Great. The guy who's going to lead us to the promised land is 15 years old and didn't even come out for basketball. I guess he's been hiding his six-foot-ten body in a study hall, waiting for you to discover him!" My skepticism was as apparent as I could make it. Mercer ignored it. His belief in his discoveries was accelerating in the face of my disbelief.

"Anteock, my boy," he said with the volume rising, "you will just have to see for yourself what I have found. The four of them will report to Levitson today, using your name as a reference when they volunteer to lift up the sagging Angler team. I have told them of your desire to bolster the sad roundball situation, and they are responding to your distress call. Any questions?" He smiled, stepped away, and looked as happy as I'd ever seen him.

"Mercer, how could you do this to me? These unknowns are going to tell Coach that I sent them? And I haven't even laid eyes on them? Can these guys even dribble? Who are they, anyway?"

By this point Mercer was laughing at my predicament. Just as he was about to respond, the bell rang for homeroom and he put himself in low gear, ready to zoom down the hall. He obviously felt no need to tell me more. I grabbed his arm and demanded, "You're not getting away from me without at least telling me the name of the 'great one' you mentioned. I'm going to hang on to you until you tell me."

Mercer's laugh turned into a smile—not that superior look I had seen previously. If I hadn't doubted that Mercer could experience it, I would have said it was a smile of joy, as he provided me with the name: "Jesse Crosse."

The day passed too fast for me. I had only two goals for the day, and I didn't know if I would accomplish either. First, I had to think of how to break the news to Coach Levitson that four players I knew nothing about were due to show up that afternoon, saying I had sent them. I spent a good deal of time in his class that morning trying to figure out what I should say about the four. I didn't want to sound like I was usurping his authority. He had already held tryouts, and none of these guys had bothered to show up. If Mercer's testimony about their skill was even remotely accurate, Coach wouldn't have cut any of them if they had tried out. I realized too late that my fuzzy plan for introducing my unearthed prospects hadn't included Mercer's intervention going so far, so fast.

I'm afraid that Mr. Levitson's discussion of Middle English lyrics in general and one in particular called "Summer Is Icumen In," was not in the forefront of my mind during English period. How was I going to explain the arrival of the four? If I didn't do it right after class, the new guys would show up and I would not have any explanation on record. Though Jewelton High School had only 150 students, give or take a few, it was big enough that Coach's path and mine might not cross again until practice. By then it would be too late. I had to talk to him, then and there.

My second objective for the day was to find out who Jesse Crosse was. There couldn't be more than 40 sophomores. Crosse had to be in that number. Being a senior, I ordinarily took little notice of sophomores. I wasn't positive I knew the name of even one. My contacts were woefully few, and I was intensely curious to get a look at the one named Crosse—Mercer's "great" find.

But my preoccupation with how to break the news gently to Coach Levitson overwhelmed my efforts to find out about Crosse. I did manage to inquire about him of three kids who said they were sophomores, but I wasn't surprised that none of them could identify him for me. I decided that since he was new that year, it made sense that he wasn't widely known. For whatever reason, even among a group as small as the sophomores, he hadn't come to the attention of anybody I talked to.

My thoughts were on Coach Levitson as I ate my lunch. When I saw him across the cafeteria, I realized I had to act. I swooped up my bologna sandwich and potato chips and stuffed them back in my sack. I had to put off eating until I could talk to Coach.

He was just breaking away from a conversation with two students as I caught up with him.

"Coach, have you got a minute?"

"Sure, Son, what can I do for you?"

I was confused about how to proceed.

"Coach, you know how we're kind of short on players?"

What a brilliant beginning! He looked at me as if I had said, "You know how we're standing in the cafeteria?" I was getting a little panicky, and I suppose that's why what came out was the truth.

"Coach, I hope you're not going to be mad at me, but I sort of recruited some players on my own. I'm sorry I didn't ask you first, but I thought we were getting sort of desperate, and I just went ahead and did it. I know I should have checked with you first, but I didn't. I'm not trying to act like I'm the coach or something, but I thought I was helping the team."

He made no sign that my confession bothered him. He merely nodded, as if inviting me to go on, which I did.

"Actually, Coach, I didn't get these guys myself. Really, it was John Mercer who found them."

At this point he did stop me with the simple question, "Who are they, Son?"

That, of course, was the thing I feared most from him. He could have told me I was getting "too big for my britches," which was a favorite phrase of his, or that I was a jerk for trying to take over his role. I really would have preferred either of those comments to his question.

"Coach, I hate to admit this, but I don't know very much about them. Mercer tells me they're all right, and they'll fit right in with your system, and he even said one guy named Jesse Crosse was pretty good. Now I know that's probably just Mercer's own personal view of things, but maybe they will be good enough to play in the j.v. games, and that wouldn't be such a bad thing, would it?"

I knew I was babbling and attempting to talk as long as possible in order to prevent him from saying anything more. I also noticed fleetingly that my taut right hand had squashed my bologna sandwich beyond the point of being able to eat it unless I closed my eyes. My nerves were getting the best of me because I remembered too well the wrath of Coach Levitson when he thought that one of "his boys" was taking on privileges that were beyond his right to exercise. All I could think of was Paul Lightman, and how he must have felt when Coach told him that he had failed. That same axe, I feared, was about to fall on me.

"Well, Son, it's kind of unusual for the manager to be getting players on his own, especially players he's never seen, and most of whose names he doesn't know, but I appreciate your efforts. When am I going to get to see these boys, or is that another thing known only to God and Mercer?"

"Known only to God and Mercer" was a remark I'd heard him use on occasion in class after one of Mercer's long disputations about one thing or another. Most of us students found it a clever, but fairly gentle put-down of Mercer, who never acknowledged it as a negative comment at all. He beamed on the few occasions when Mr. Levitson let it fly.

"As it happens, Coach," I said with relief and gratitude for the lightness of his remark, "the four guys are scheduled to report to you after school today. You understand that I didn't promise Mercer that they would automatically be on the team. They'll have to measure up to your standards, of course."

The Coach could tell, no doubt, that I was backing off as best as I could from the role of secret talent scout and self-appointed assistant coach.

"Of course! I know you're only trying to help the old Angler cause, although that comment I made the other day about you having to practice may have had a little bit to do with your enthusiasm to rustle up some subs, didn't it?"

I realized that the man knew me all too well. I grinned and admitted that maybe there was something to his interpretation. I felt forgiven for what I thought was a transgression against a man who had always treated me well. I promised myself that I wouldn't act in important team matters without consulting him first—a promise I later deeply regretted breaking.

"Son, since you're partly responsible for these young men, why don't you come over to the gym this afternoon on the off-chance that Mercer, who is well known for his talk, might really be sending us some people. You can shag balls and give me your opinion of the results of your recruiting venture."

My heart had resumed its regular pattern of beating after what was undeniably some heavy-duty pounding, and I assured Coach that I would be on hand to do whatever he wanted when the four boys arrived. I felt that what could have been a major blunder on my part had been limited to a minor misjudgment because of Coach Levitson's generous nature.

All that remained was to see if the Mercer quartet could perform reasonable impersonations of basketball players, and I thought briefly about Crosse, the "great" prospect. The crisis with Coach Levitson being resolved, however, Jesse Crosse faded from my mind as I wondered whether I could bear to eat the mangled bologna sandwich for lunch.

CHAPTER FOUR

I had intended to go to the gym as soon as school was over, but I was delayed slightly by a conversation, a conversation that I saw as essential to my social development. When my sense of duty finally prevailed, I bid farewell to her (the one with whom I hoped to be more social) and hurried to see the results of Mercer's talent search. When I got to the gym, there were only six or seven young kids, ninth-graders I supposed, who were hanging around, maybe killing time waiting for a ride or simply putting off their departure for home by hurling shots at the baskets. When I got to Coach Levitson's office, he was alone. The foursome was apparently in no hurry to show up. I wondered if they would.

The Coach greeted me with, "Luke, what do you think?"

"About what, Coach?"

"The new boys—didn't you see them when you came in? You must have walked right by them. I told them to warm up for a couple of minutes, and then I'd give them a look-see."

I knew right then that Mercer had done his worst. His eccentric view of things had prompted him to grab four nondescript kids and foist them off on us. I tried to remember what anybody out in the gym looked like. I was searching for something in my memory that just wasn't there. Someone tall? Somebody who was making a long-range jump shot? Nothing. Just some very short, very young-looking boys.

I felt as if I should say something, so I began to alibi: "Oh, I was in such a hurry, Coach, that I really didn't notice who was in the gym. The Celtics could have been working out and I probably would have missed them."

He smiled patiently, seeing through my excuse. He understood that I felt responsible in some measure for the presence of the recruits, and he wanted to take me off the hook.

"They aren't the Celtics, that's for sure. Now, Luke, don't worry if this doesn't work out. We'll just spend a couple of minutes seeing what they can do, and then it will all be over. I promise you that no matter what happens, I won't draft you on to the team."

"Thanks, Coach, but I really wasn't concerned about that so much; I'm afraid that this is just going to be a big waste of time for you and for those kids out there."

His reply was typical of him: "It won't hurt to spend a little time with these boys. After all, they're willing to try to help us, so we owe them a fair chance to show what they're capable of. Let's go see what they've got."

When we returned to the gym floor, all the boys except four had vanished, as if on cue. Since Coach Levitson was not possessive about the use of the gymnasium by students who were not players on the team, he would not have cleared the place for our "tryout." The prospect of other boys watching our pitiful attempt to round up more players would have embarrassed me. I was grateful for their departure.

"Boys, come on down to this basket," the Coach said. Coming at us from the distance, they looked to be four of the shortest guys I had ever imagined as high school basketball players. I hoped somehow that as they got closer they would seem to grow. They didn't. They were as short when they got to the Coach and me as they appeared to be from 90 feet away.

"Now let me see who we've got here." Coach was holding a clipboard with a list of drills that he used at the beginning of practice sessions. He was preparing to write their names down—an exercise that struck me as pointless. But I supposed he wanted to give them the impression that he was going through all the usual procedures. It was thoughtful of him, but I saw it as merely putting off his inevitable decision that we couldn't use them on the team.

"Tell me your names and what grade you're in, will you, boys?" The Coach readied his ballpoint as they stepped forward. They lined up single file, almost as if they had practiced for this moment. I was rather touched by their silent ritual. These four little guys were volunteering for our team. It reminded me of pictures I had seen of teen-aged boys of various countries being inducted into the army for a nation on the verge of losing a war. They began to identify themselves:

"Si Montler, 11th grade," said the first of them, a pale blonde boy who had the dubious distinction of being the tallest of the group at about 5'7". He was followed by two others, even shorter, who announced that they also were juniors. Their names were Phil Lipscomb and Bart Holeman. Finally, and it then dawned on me, was Mercer's choice as the best of the bunch:

"Jesse Crosse, 10th grade."

This was said by what was no doubt the shortest, blackest boy that the 10th grade had to offer. The description of him that occurred to me at the time still lingers: "Five-feet-three and a hundred-and-three." Both, I still believe, were accurate. As regards his race, over the passage of years I have learned to use the word *black* in referring to people I used to call Negroes. It is apparently the general preference of people who are African-American, and I follow it as a courtesy to them, much as I would pronounce a man's name as he would like it to be said. But even in 1960 the word "black" would have been the first to spring to my mind in describing Jesse Crosse.

I was surprised on first seeing him that my inquiries about him had turned up nothing, because he was distinctive for the purity of his blackness; he was ebony, jet, or whatever adjective best describes the state in its perfection of containing all colors. He, like the others, seemed strikingly shy and uncomfortable in identifying himself. Crosse cradled the ball against his hip, and waited with his three diminutive comrades for Coach Levitson to speak.

The Coach gave me the impression that he was sizing them up, and considering their size, it occurred to me that the process was going far over the time it should take. He finally broke the weighty silence by introducing me: "Boys, this is Luke Anteock, our manager, whose efforts have brought you here today. He's going to help me run you through your paces. First thing I want you to do is to line up for a layup drill."

I could tell from the four uncomprehending faces that they weren't sure what to do. When Mercer told me that they had never played organized basketball before, I never conceived that they would be so unfamiliar with its routines that they wouldn't know how to arrange themselves to shoot layups. They had apparently exhausted their lining-up technique when they told Coach their names. The Coach detected their problem and asked them to go to the center of the court on the right side of the basket and to make basketball's shortest shot while running to the basket. They did seem to understand what he wanted, although I could tell that none of them wanted to be the first to go for the goal. Crosse looked inquiringly at me as if for a cue, and I motioned to him to pass me the ball. Instead he came over to me and placed it in my hands, as if making sure that he did not err in his first act of the tryout. He then ran to the end of what was, in more ways than one, a very short line.

I stood under the basket and told the one called Si, who had ended up first in the line, perhaps because he had already braved the position once, to run toward me and take his shot. Si made the basket. There was nothing remarkable in that. But what startled me was his speed. Si could really run! I had intended to lob him the ball far enough away from the basket so that he would have to dribble a time or two before taking the shot. But he was so quick that by the time my pass got to him, he was close enough to the goal to merely take the allotted two steps and put up the shot. That was my first surprise. The fact that Lipscomb, Holeman, and Crosse were equally quick and were all able to take the shot without dribbling amazed me even more. I had to concede one thing to Mercer. Although the four might not make the Jewelton basketball team, he had recruited the nucleus for an excellent track team—if only we had one!

After gathering in Crosse's successful first shot, I took a glance at Coach Levitson to see his reaction, but his face was impassive. I could detect nothing at all. The boys had returned to their original spots on the floor, and each had a grin on his face. I was determined to get them the ball earlier the second time, to force a dribble. Montler waited with a look of anticipation on his face, not daring to take off until I indicated that he was to do so. His attitude, and that of the others, was such that I felt they viewed me as an official figure in the proceedings. Perhaps they considered me important since Coach had mentioned that I was instrumental in getting them the opportunity to perform that afternoon.

"Let's go!" I barked at Montler, and as soon as he headed for the basket, I fired him a bounce pass that wasn't very well aimed. In my desire to be certain that he get the pass sooner rather than later, I let fly with what looked like a throw that would skid by him to his left. Montler made a lightning adjustment in his own path and cleanly fielded the ball. He was then out of line to go to the goal, but he rapidly dribbled back to the direction he had initially taken. His dribble was low, fast, and sure. He made a beeline for the goal at what I thought was a rate equal to his first try and laid that shot in, too.

I was impressed, not only with the first of the four, but with them all. They were faster dribbling the ball than any of our regular players were running without it. After a few more shots, Coach Levitson told me to try them from the left side, and they did just as well from there. I noted with satisfaction that they all shot those layups with the left hand, something I had seen the Coach painstakingly try to teach many of his players over the years. As far as he was concerned, it was the only correct way to take that shot. They had probably made about five each from the left when Coach moved in.

"All right, boys, now I want you to try some jump shots from out on the floor. Since you're obviously not trying out for center, you'll have to shoot a few long ones now and then."

Was I hearing things? The Coach sounded as if they had already made the team! I knew that they had been impressive in the layup drill, but they hadn't shot more than 10 times each. He was talking as if they were a cinch to make the team. I liked what I had seen too, but I wasn't putting an Angler jersey on them yet. The irony of this did not escape me. I, who had hoped that somehow the foursome would pan out, was now making mental reservations about considering them team members. Maybe Coach was more desperate than I had imagined. I supposed the thought of avoiding the forfeiture of the junior varsity games had caused him to ease up on his usual standards.

He pointed to the top of the free-throw circle as the spot where he wanted the boys to shoot from next. It was about 20 feet from the basket. Then an odd thing happened. The four of them stood their ground, as if unwilling to go to the point he had indicated. They looked worried, each one of them, as if Coach had asked them to do something that was against their religion. They glanced at each other for support. Then Crosse stepped forward. His voice was soft and respectful, but it was firm: "Coach, we don't shoot from that far out. We can't make that shot." He then took a step back with the others, as if expecting a rebuke. I expected something too, although I wasn't sure what. Would the Coach berate Crosse for his audacity? Would he laugh at the preposterous declaration? Anybody would have been able to tell the four squatty bodies that it was essential for a little man to be able to at least take such a shot as part of his repertoire. Little guys don't get layups exclusively. As a matter of fact, the number of such shots that the typical Angler got in a season could usually be counted on one hand. I waited for the Coach's reaction.

"You're absolutely right, Son. It's a very poor shot to take, and most teams would be better off if they never bothered with it. I've seen enough, I guess. If you want to join the team, our first practice of the year is next Monday right after school. Luke, put the ball away, will you?"

The astonishment that I felt was surpassed only by the thrill that the Coach's words evidently brought to the little band. They smiled hugely, and patted each other on the back. It wasn't until then that I really took notice of the fact that not one of them was wearing anything remotely like decent basketball shoes. Their footgear, although no doubt once intended for the hardwood sport, was battered and worn from exposure to something much rougher than the wood court at Jewelton High. I was wondering about several things at that moment, but one question that persisted was how much better they might be able to move with the traction which new shoes could provide.

The four of them bolted from the gym, with Crosse getting my attention and wonderment one last time. Just before darting out the door, and as if struck by a sudden idea, he abruptly turned and waved goodbye to me.

CHAPTER FIVE

I had seen Coach Mo Levitson in many moods, but never like the one I found him in when I entered his office to put away the basketball. It was probably more what he didn't say than what he said that clued me in to his extraordinary state of mind. He made no comment to me whatsoever as I placed the ball in the canvas duffle bag we kept our supply in, and I felt compelled to make some kind of comment.

"Pretty speedy, aren't they?" I offered.

He was gazing out his office window in the direction of the trees which surrounded Lake Tiberias, and he seemed as if he didn't hear me. I tried again. "Those guys were all pretty fast, weren't they, Coach?" Again, there was no response. Then he turned to me with a suddenness that surprised me.

"Luke, where on earth do you suppose Mercer found them? I think I knew the Montler and Holeman boys to see them, and I believe I remember a Lipscomb girl who was a student here a few years back, and he may be her brother, but where has Crosse been? It's not as if we have such a large school that he could easily be overlooked. I've never even laid eyes on the boy, and he'd be hard to miss, now wouldn't he?" Coach gave me the impression of a man pondering an impossible idea: a square circle. He further appeared to be unwilling to let the difficult concept go, as many a person might do, once it became clear that no answer was forthcoming.

What I was interested in more than where the four came from was how, in 10 minutes or fewer, he had decided to accept them. I acknowledged the fact that they were fleet, but I couldn't see that alone as good reason for so readily embracing them. And what about Crosse's refusal, for the entire group, to shoot the long shot? And why had Coach given in so easily to that refusal? It didn't make sense to me. I tried to discover his perceptions by asking, "So what did you think of them?" It was no use. He was lost in thought again. He blinked at me as if he recognized that I had addressed him and said, "Fastest feet we've ever had. And good hands. How the heck did Mercer find them and I didn't?"

I could tell that I was making no progress in my inquiry, because all we seemed to be doing was asking each other questions that the other wouldn't or couldn't answer. I made one last attempt to break into his reverie: "Coach, should I get out practice uniforms for those guys and make entries in the equipment file?"

This interrogatory eventually made its way to his response center. Not that it was accomplished quickly. It hung in the air as if frozen, and then suddenly popped through to his consciousness. He glanced at me with a big grin, and happily announced, "Those boys will be needing jerseys and shorts on Monday, Luke. See to that, will you? I've got to say this for you and Mercer, you've certainly given me something to think about over the weekend."

I had no clear idea of what was going to be on Coach Levitson's mind, but I knew what, or who, was on my mind. It was Mercer. I wanted information from him.

I didn't know where to find Mercer on a Friday night. After supper, I excused myself from the table and started hunting through the telephone directory. There were a couple of Mercers listed, but I could tell from the addresses that they were both in town, and Mercer lived somewhere out in the country. I called Johnny Wirges, who was not only my long-standing good friend, but was the kind of person who paid attention to little details about people. He was uncommonly friendly and genuinely interested in others. I guessed that he might know where Mercer, the lone wolf, lived.

Johnny not only knew where Mercer lived, he volunteered to drive me out to his house. He told me that the Mercers had no telephone, and that if I wanted to talk to him, the only way was to "take the journey," as he put it. My mother and father were not the type to make me beg to go out; they only required that I ask, rather than presume, permission. They found my request to hunt down Mercer as a bit unusual, since I had never before mentioned wanting to see him. They knew from my comments about school and my classmates that Mercer was in the "oddball" category as far as I was concerned. Nevertheless, they said OK, and I got ready for Johnny's arrival.

He was punctual as usual, and we set out for Mercer's. Johnny was probably curious about my reasons for wanting to see Mercer, but he didn't ask. I was eager to share with him the events of that afternoon, however, and he was soon as amazed as I was by the performance of the four and Coach Levitson's reaction to them. Johnny, a senior, had been an Angler since the 10th grade, and had an obvious stake in the addition of four guys to contend for playing time.

"So they just shot a few layups and that was it?" he summarized. "It sure is weird. I guess he saw something you didn't. He's got more than 20 years' experience, you know."

I knew. But that didn't make it any easier for me to understand. As we left the limits of Jewelton and headed east, Johnny filled me in on some things about Mercer I didn't know. He lived with his aunt. He was perhaps the poorest student in our school, and his bony appearance was probably due to a diet that was deficient. There were even rumors that he and his aunt were sometimes forced to hunt to feed themselves, and that they ate various dishes which his aunt prepared from wildflowers and other unusual plant life.

Five minutes after we left Highway 21, Johnny told me that we were getting close to Mercer's. Then we made another turn on to a dirt road, and an isolated house was at the end of it. It was a sad place, as ramshackle as Johnny's description of Mercer's economic situation had led me to believe it would be. As we approached, I realized that the lights of Johnny's car were illuminating a darkened house. As we came to a stop, I asked Johnny, "Do you think there's anybody home?"

"Oh, yeah. They're there. There isn't any other place for them to be. I'll just honk, and he'll come out. I've been here once before, and that's what I did last time." And so he sounded his horn, and in a second or two Mercer was on the porch.

"Who's there?" he yelled in a challenging voice. There was a threat in this throat which warned anyone that here was a young man on his home territory, and he meant to protect his interests.

"Wirges and Anteock." Johnny shouted. "Luke wants to talk to you about the players you found for him. Coach Levitson liked 'em a lot. Come on out."

Mercer bounded off the ancient porch, apparently keen to talk. He sidled up to the driver's side and exchanged hellos with Johnny. I could tell that even the acerbic Mercer liked Johnny Wirges. He bent slightly to see me in the shotgun seat and triumphantly crowed, "So Levitson liked them, did he? I'm not surprised. As a matter of fact, I knew he'd be crazy about them."

"He's crazy, all right." I interjected, "They barely even worked up a sweat before he put them on the team. What I want to know is where you found them. What's the background on these guys? If it weren't for the fact that they didn't even know how to run a layup drill, I'd swear they'd been playing a lot of basketball somewhere before."

Mercer noted accurately: "That's a whole bunch of stuff for me to deal with at one time, Anteock. But I'll be happy to fill you in. I'll try to take it in the order you gave it to me. First of all, they're off the junior high playground. Nobody thinks to look over there for high school basketball players, but the truth is that because of their size, it's the only place where they can ever get a court. The two outside courts at school are dominated by would-be football players who can't play basketball for spit, but they can manage to keep off smaller guys—which they do. And the courts in the gym seemed just too fancy for that modest quartet. So that humble group has been relegated to the court of the younger set. They've only been playing there for about three weeks. Somehow they just came together, although I'm convinced that Crosse had something to do with it. It's like he walked around for a couple of days after school started, and then picked out the other three. I'm sure it happened that way, though nobody ever told me so."

Mercer's pleasure at telling this tale was evident, because he scarcely took a breath as he continued non-stop: "Now the amazing thing about these guys is that when they're on the court together with nobody around to play them, they don't play each other two-on-two. Instead they work with each other, as a unit. The junior high kids found out fast enough that there was nothing to be gained from challenging them to play. They just got massacred trying to keep up with those four. So they have spent the better part of three weeks just working out— and I stress this word, *together*. Did you happen to notice their shoes?"

I barely got a chance to nod before he rambled on: "I happen to know, because I asked, that they have worn them out in a mere three weeks. Those guys can really burn it up! Now tell me, Anteock, have you ever seen a faster bunch?"

Once again he didn't wait for my answer, which would have been in the negative. Mercer took a slight gasp for air and then added, "These four will make a difference, Anteock, mark my words. And Crosse is the one we've all been waiting for—our 'great' Negro ballplayer. But it'll probably take time before you, much less anybody else, recognize it. Levitson knows it though. That old keeper of the flame of pure basketball knows in his heart of hearts that he has found what has eluded him all these years."

I guessed that Mercer was as thrilled as he was about the four because they were his discoveries. His predictions about Jesse Crosse were beyond me, however. I knew as well as Mercer did that many people were either openly or quietly hoping for a black player who would lend his unique, and what some thought was racial, talent to the Anglers. But Jesse Crosse wouldn't have been what people had in mind. There was no way that he could fit the image of the player who could save Jewelton.

As if he sensed my doubts, Mercer quickly added, "Anteock, what else did

Levitson have them do besides layups before he took them on?"

For the first time he paused long enough for me to comment: "That was it. It was over in a flash."

This evoked a joyful look and he radiated good feelings as he chirped, "Then neither you nor Levitson has seen the ultimate gift that Crosse has to offer. To put it as briefly as possible, the boy can work miracles with a basketball! You'll see what I mean."

I could tell that as far as Mercer was concerned the conversation was over. As he stepped away from Johnny's door, he asked me, "So, Doc, have you got what you came for?"

His use of "Doc" surprised me. It sounded like a softening of his attitude toward me, the unbeliever. Having no nickname to use in return, I simply said, "Thanks, John. That's plenty. I'll let you know how practice goes Monday."

"You won't have to do that," said a grinning Mercer, "I'll be in the front row of the bleachers to see it for myself!"

Johnny started the engine, said goodbye, and turned the car around. As we headed back home, we discussed the meeting with Mercer. We didn't know what to make of his wild predictions. As Johnny let me off at my house he said, "I'm eager to see Crosse and the other guys on Monday, aren't you?" I was.

CHAPTER SIX

I had mixed feelings as Monday's practice drew near. For one thing, I still doubted the wisdom of Coach Levitson's hasty decision. On the other hand, I was hoping that he knew a great deal more than I did about the newcomers' talents. After all, I had taken a part in their enlistment, and I was selfishly viewing their possible assistance to the Anglers as a personal contribution to our team's success. Another thought occurred to me over the weekend that didn't comfort me. What if the established players resented the intrusion of the new team members? Perhaps the influx of more players would be a slap in the face to those already on the team. Would they think of it as a blunt suggestion that they couldn't get the job done? I decided to try to quit worrying about all the various angles and Anglers, if I could—and just let the chips fall where they may.

At practice, the chips did begin to fall. With Mercer in the second row of bleacher seats as the only onlooker besides me, Coach Levitson greeted 13 boys at approximately 3:45 with the words: "We're going to make some changes this year."

I could tell that the guys who had previously been on the team were immediately suspicious. They exchanged puzzled, disapproving glances and then stared at the new foursome. No doubt some or all of the veterans had heard, prior to practice, of the recent additions. They hadn't appeared curious about the four boys who were warming up together at a side goal before Coach Levitson arrived. They ignored them. But I was convinced that they were very aware of them.

I had abandoned my usual departure for the dressing room, determined not to miss a thing. After issuing the balls from the duffle bag, I slouched in the bleachers opposite Mercer, acting as casually as I could. But I could see the two distinct groups, one more than twice the size of the other, and this raised my level of apprehension. Even Johnny Wirges, whom I might have expected to break the ice with the little group, remained steadfastly aligned with the other eight regular players. They warmed up at the main goal at the opposite end from Mercer's recruits.

After Coach had made his announcement, he quickly began practice. Every first practice of the Anglers that I had ever witnessed had begun with layups. But not today. He put the players in four groups and stipulated that they were to sprint from one end of the court to the other, as fast as they could go. The "old timers" looked shocked, but the newly-arrived quartet showed no reaction at all, since they didn't know that this was a novel procedure. Coach read off the names of the members of each group, trusting to information on the clipboard rather than his memory. At once I recognized that he had placed one new boy in each group. He was going to have them succeed at something from the start. And did they succeed! First Holeman, then Crosse, then Montler, and then Lipscomb ran away from the others in their respective groups. Time after time they went up and down the court. It was painfully obvious in a few minutes that the distance between the winner of each group and his competitors was growing larger and larger.

The four little guys were not only superior in speed, they were in much better shape. Some of the regulars began to lag so far behind as the sprints continued that it was almost embarrassing. The face of the nine began to contort with effort, while Crosse and the others gulped air with apparently cavernous lungs and kept up their blistering pace. I began to wonder if Coach was ever going to let up. My guess is that each group ran 30 dashes the full length of the gym. Some of the out-of-shape gang began to clutch at their sides, and then Pete Barjon, considered the best athlete of them all, threw up.

Pete not only vomited, he fell to the floor on his hands and knees in the very place where he had gotten sick. Repulsed though I was by the situation, I knew that this was what a manager and trainer was for: to assist a player in need. Coach Levitson ignored Pete, except to check that I was on my way to help him. By then he had blown the whistle and was explaining that the conditioning program of past years would not compare with what he had planned for the present season. As I neared Pete, I saw his brother Andy and Johnny Wirges exchange glances which I interpreted to mean that they were already fully aware that a big change had taken place.

I knelt next to Pete, getting no closer than duty required, and I could see that his eyes were glazy, and he was still feeling terrible. Through lips that were not pleasant to look at, he choked, "Damn it, Doc! What's he trying to do to do, kill us?" I had never seen Pete brought so low. Ordinarily he was the rock on our team. He was the one who never gave up. He was the staunchest of all the Anglers, a player whose talent was not great, but whose heart was. He alone was capable of winning the respect of fans from other schools. They may have derided the Jewelton team, but Pete's heroic refusal to play less than all-out, even when the Anglers were getting clobbered, never failed to evoke admiration. The sight of him all but crawling in his own rejected lunch was shocking to me, and to his old teammates too, of that I was sure.

By bringing Pete to his knees with the first drill, Coach Levitson had served notice that a dramatic shift had taken place. The past, with its reliable elements, was a goner. I suspected that Coach knew Pete would drive himself to something like this. His competitive spirit just didn't know when to yield. Instead of pacing himself in the sprints as the other eight began to do, Pete only ran the harder. He was fortunate to be grouped with Tom Dubius, who was slower than he, but cursed to have to try to stay with Crosse. The sight of the skinny black kid streaking down court ahead of him had prodded Pete to try to find a reservoir of speed and stamina he simply didn't have. No, Coach didn't accidently put Pete up against Crosse. If the new, coal-black, 10th grader could run Pete into submission, then all the players, old and new, would re-examine their assumptions about who was in and who was out. There was much more to basketball than running up and down the court, but running was one measure of athletic prowess, and Jesse Crosse had totally demolished Pete Barjon's reputation as the one who would be standing after all others had fallen.

I helped Pete to his feet and cleaned him up the best I could. He was in need of being steadied as he walked, and I marveled at his fragile condition compared to that of Crosse, who at that moment I saw zooming to the goal to sink a layup in the drill that had returned the Angler practice to a familiar form. "Doc, I need a swig of water. If I'm going back out there, I'll have to replace some of what I just threw up." This declaration from Pete assured me that his competitive spark was not extinguished. Any other player of the established group would probably have checked it in for the day after such an upheaval, but I knew that Pete was constitutionally unable to back off from the challenge he had been handed.

We staggered to the fountain; he took a few swallows, walked a bit, discarded his befouled sweat shirt, and ran back on the floor to join the drills. He pulled up in line behind Jim Wirges, Johnny's brother, who turned and looked at him grimly. I surmised that Pete had lost more than his lunch. If Jim's expression was any indication, Pete's old teammates were not as sure of his status as they once were.

The next drill was a familiar one too. It was intended to simulate the fast break, an offensive play which the Anglers practice often, but rarely were able to execute in games. It consisted of Coach Levitson taking a shot which he purposely would miss. The object was to have one player rebound the miss and for the other four to take off at full speed for the opposite goal. It wasn't just a matter of helter-skelter running, however. Each player had a specific route to run. The idea was that when the other team fired up an errant try for the goal, the Anglers would race down the floor and make an easy shot before the other team's defense had time to assemble. As I stated, it was something that Coach Levitson required the team to practice, but we just couldn't seem to make it work under game conditions.

Coach assigned five veterans to run the drill. He put together two of our "brother" combinations. One thing that was distinctive about the Jewelton team was its three sets of brothers, the Barjon and Wirges brothers and the Alpheson boys, Jude and Jimmy. The Alphesons and Barjons were joined by Matt Tachsman for the fast break. Coach Levitson said nothing to the four short sprinters by way of explanation as to how the drill was to be run. They stood on the sidelines and watched as the first quintet methodically went through the procedure without a hitch. They looked like they could run it in their sleep. The only problem was that it wasn't a very "fast" fast break. Even though the guys all knew their roles, they didn't carry them out with much verve. Maybe they were just exhausted from all the other running. Coach tried several combinations without ever using the four, who were watching the action very closely.

Then, after various groups of veterans made trips up and down the floor, Coach Levitson called "Holeman, Crosse, Montler, and Lipscomb" to the court, and assigned Johnny Wirges to be the fifth player. Still there was no explanation to the new players about what to do. The shot was missed, and the five took off. What chaos! They ran every-which-way. They scrambled all over the court. What they did was fast, but the only "break" would have been what such a play would have given the opposing team. The eight holdover players who were stationed next to the court could hardly restrain their laughter. Johnny Wirges looked pleadingly at Coach Levitson to be removed from the confusion. Still, Coach proposed no solution to the disorder. He only barked out four new names to join Wirges. Crosse and his mates quickly got off the court. Were they humiliated by their performance? Their faces showed no emotion as they became spectators again. All I saw was an intensity in their observation. Not two minutes passed before Coach put them together with Wirges again.

As the shot rebounded from the rim, I tried to figure out what Coach was up to. What was the point of making the new players look good in the sprints, and then making them look stupid in this drill? The rebound went to Montler, who turned and fired a pass to Lipscomb on the sidelines, exactly where he should have been. He dribbled twice, then flipped the ball to Crosse, who was already in high gear approaching the center line. In front of him on the right was Holeman, and to his left and ahead was Johnny. I said Crosse was in "high gear" when he caught Lipscomb's pass, but that must have been inaccurate, for when he took off down the center of the floor dribbling, he accelerated even more. Perhaps the correct automotive term for that increase at what already appeared to be top speed is that he shifted into "overdrive." As Crosse blazed for the goal, I saw that Holeman and Johnny were too far ahead of him for the break to work successfully. Usually the "point" man on the break, which was Crosse at that moment, was to pass to a player on either his right or left for an easy, close basket. But Holeman and Wirges were going to run completely off the court before Crosse could get the ball to them. It was a problem with the fast break that I had seen the Anglers struggle with unsuccessfully on many occasions. Crosse seemed so intent on his full-speed dribble that I figured he wouldn't see the two in front of him until it was too late to do anything about it.

As I look back at that moment in practice, I realize that was when I understood for the first time what Mercer meant about Jesse Crosse's "gift." Crosse was about to find himself alone on the court. Holeman and Johnny were too far ahead down the sidelines. Then he sharply shifted his head in Holeman's direction. Maybe he did have time to get Holeman the ball, after all. And then the pass was made. Perfect! Right on target. Exactly at waist level. The layup was an easy two points. What was not easy, what in fact was impossible, was to believe that it was Johnny, not Holeman, who was the recipient of the dart that Crosse had thrown. Without even looking at him, Crosse had thrown Johnny a 30-foot pass, from behind his back!

It is to Johnny's credit that he did not blow the layup. To have the most spectacular pass ever thrown in the Jewelton gym lead to anything less than a successful shot would have been a pity. But how Johnny managed it, not even he knew. Later, when asked about it, he said the oddest thing:

"I don't even remember taking the shot."

How could he forget? With no hesitation, or any indication of surprise, Johnny had gathered in the ball and had smoothly and calmly put it against the backboard and through the rim. When he turned from under the goal where his momentum had carried him, Johnny was possessed of a smile that reminded me of Mercer's look of joy. No one said anything. The silence was total but for the light splat of the leather ball bouncing lower and lower after easing through the net. Everyone was still. Coach Levitson had the whistle to his lips, but he didn't use it. He was staring at Jesse Crosse, who was looking back at the Coach questioningly, waiting for further instructions. Just then I happened to glance in the direction of Mercer, his smile a mile wide, and he winked at me and his right thumb pointed to the ceiling.

Then Coach managed a kind of strangled peep through his whistle. He blurted something about that being enough for one day, and that everyone should make 50 free throws before leaving. He then did something he'd never done before. He left the court before his players. He headed straight for his office without looking back. I thought that perhaps he was sick or something, so I followed him. By the time I got to his office, he had done something else totally out of character: He had closed his door, and I heard him lock it.

CHAPTER SEVEN

I didn't find out what was on Coach's mind as Monday's practice came to a close, but I learned a lot about what the nine veteran players thought when we got back to the locker room.

As if by unspoken agreement, the nine delayed their leaving long enough so that Crosse, Lipscomb, Montler, and Holeman left first. I was puzzled and a little upset by Coach's behavior, but also nearly jubilant about how the session had ended, as Crosse's incredible pass was still fresh in my mind. The mood of the nine was easier to describe: They were unhappy.

J.I. Tradeau, who was known to everyone only by his last name, voiced the first complaint as soon as the four new players were gone. "What I want to know is why we have to put up with this! I say that we go to Levitson right now and let him know that he's not going to kill us just so he can watch four midgets run wild." Tradeau delivered his ultimatum to a group whose weariness may have accounted for the absence of an enthusiastic response. Tradeau looked confused by the fact that he drew no second to his motion, and he adopted a more democratic tone: "What do you guys think we ought to do?"

Andy Barjon, who was accustomed to following his older brother's lead, looked at the haggard Pete slumping on the bench by his locker, and decided to speak for himself. "Tradeau, you know what Levitson would do if we tried something like that. He'd kick us all off the team, get Doc a jersey, and play with just five guys for the rest of the season. I don't like what happened out there any more than you do, but we've got to come up with a better solution than the one you just made." Tradeau looked deflated by Andy's words, and he muttered something to himself and began to take his clothes from his locker. There was silence. Everyone was waiting for the emergence of the better suggestion than Andy had called for.

"I don't object to getting in shape," Jim Alpheson said, "but I can't understand why it has to be done in one day." Then he brought up what was the sensitive matter of Pete's collapse. "Levitson never did anything like this before. He nearly killed Pete by putting him up against that colored kid. I think it's all just a big plan of his to show us how out of shape we are. I doubt if he really intends to keep those four guys anyway. He just brought them in to run our legs off for a few days, so we'd realize how much work we had to do before we were ready to play ball. Did you notice that he stopped practice before they had to do much besides run and shoot layups? I was watching them shoot free throws, and not one of them looked any good to me."

This interpretation of events by Jim seemed to satisfy everyone. There were a couple of assenting remarks, and soon the locker room was empty except for Pete, who had not even showered. I had to be the last to leave, since a key managerial duty was to lock the gym. I didn't know how Pete felt, since he hadn't said a word. He lifted his head and questioned me. "Doc, I hear that you and Mercer found those guys. Is that right?" I indicated that it was, and he continued, "Did coach tell you to go out and flush out four jackrabbits, so we'd get in shape faster?" He was testing Jim's theory.

"No, Pete, as a matter of fact, he didn't even know we were looking for players. At least I don't think he did. He could have had something already agreed upon with Mercer, but I don't think so. I think he was really surprised when I told him four guys were going to try out for the team." Pete nodded at what I had to say. Wearily he commented, "I didn't think Jim knew what he was talking about. Those four shrimps may not shoot very well, but they can get up and down the floor. I thought that little Negro kid was going to wear me out." He had to smile weakly at what he'd just said. "Hell, he did wear me out! I'd put my head down waiting for Coach's whistle, and when he blew it, I'd bust my gut to keep up with that guy. I'd swear he had a five-yard head start on every one of those sprints. But I guess he didn't, huh?"

He could tell from my look that Jesse hadn't jumped the gun. He shook his head sadly. "Doc, I stunk in more ways than one today. At least now I know how out of shape I am. Even if Coach only wants to use those four little rockets to run our tails off, I can see how much ahead of the rest of us they are. None of us can go as fast as they can, but, I swear, we can all do a whole lot better at keeping up with them than we did today." As he lifted himself from the bench with obvious effort, I had to bring up the performance of Jesse Crosse.

"Pete, you saw what Crosse did on that behind-the-back pass. Everybody did. How come nobody said anything about it?" I couldn't understand why it had been so universally ignored. Pete turned from his trip to the showers and gave me a puzzling answer. "Maybe we just couldn't believe our eyes. Or didn't want to."

★★★★★

Whatever got into Coach Levitson that caused him to end Monday's practice so abruptly, it was gone by the next day. As a matter of fact, I'd describe him as positively cheery as we began our second day of getting ready for the season. His first order was met with mostly sullen faces when he started with the sprints again. This time, however, he made no specific assignments. The veteran players quickly sought out each other to avoid having to compete against the "jackrabbits." Pete was the exception. He found Jesse Crosse to run with. Montler, Lipscomb, and Holeman ended up running against each other. It was typical of Pete to want to run with Crosse. He had to demonstrate to the others perhaps, but to himself for sure, that he would not dodge the challenge of the black speedster.

There were only 10 sprints that day. Everyone held up markedly better than he had the day before, especially since only Pete was pitted against one of the "rockets." Crosse won every trip down the floor, but Pete managed to stay within shouting distance of him. It was a far more respectable showing, and, to my relief, no one threw up. After two or three more drills, Coach sounded his whistle and gathered the team about him. He looked them over before speaking, as if gauging his audience, "Boys, we've used the same offensive plays for years. We know them like the backs of our hands. That's good. What's not so good is that our opponents know those plays by now too. If you've sometimes felt that they knew exactly what we were going to do, that's because they did. As of today, we're going to install a new offense that will bedazzle our fans and bewilder our opponents." Coach's use of "bedazzle" and "bewilder" I recognized as a literary technique known as alliteration. He had taught us about it in American Literature. It was supposed to be pleasing to the ear to hear repetitions of consonant sounds like that, but I detected that quite a number of his listeners were not pleased at all. It was evident that the one obvious advantage that the nine had over the four was being eliminated. The fact that the four newcomers didn't know Coach's old offensive sets was one stumbling block for them that I had speculated about. How could they catch up with the others as long as they were behind with regard to knowing the plays? Now it didn't matter that they were ignorant, because everybody else was equally ignorant.

As I looked around at the players hearing this announcement, I noted some surprise and chagrin, and Tradeau's expression came close to what I'd call resentment. Coach paused to let his words sink in, although it wasn't necessary. The players knew right away what the repercussions were. No one held an edge on anyone else any more. They were all starting even.

But coach was not through dropping bombshells. "One other thing I want you boys to think about is this. You know how the lineups usually work out. Five boys get to start, and two or three others usually get a little bit of time playing as substitutes. I'm going to change that too. I want you to begin thinking in terms of units—two groups that will play about the same amount of time in each game. I know it's going to take some getting used to, but I think you'll like it when you see what it does for our team. So now it's time to learn our new bedazzling and bewildering offense."

His attempt to evoke some enthusiasm for his revamped plans had generally fallen on deaf ears; that was apparent. Most of our veterans looked stunned. The old system probably would have been just fine with them when there were only nine players. There would have been five who had the lion's share of playing time, and it was probably easy for each of the nine to imagine himself as one of those starters. It was as if they had become old-timers at 17; the group of nine was that set in its ways. The radical changes of Coach Levitson were going to meet resistance.

Coach was oblivious to any reluctance on their part, however, and began to position them on the floor and to explain the details of their duties to them. The excitement in his voice was unmistakable. I felt a bit guilty and somewhat overwhelmed when I realized that if I had never talked to Mercer, none of what was unfolding would have been taking place. That intervention was to be the significant part, for good or for ill, that I played in the events of that year.

As I analyzed what was happening on the gym floor that afternoon, I concluded that Coach Levitson had fashioned an attack based on speed and an extraordinary number of passes. It was an offense that tried to do two things that were almost opposites. First, he intended for the Anglers to run the fast break in earnest. It was no longer just a practice exercise. He wanted the players to accept the fact that he was committed to it as a primary way that Jewelton would score points that year. Second, if the fast break did not materialize, the Anglers would then go to offensive patterns that called for pass after pass after pass before the shot was taken. And all five players were always on the move. He used the word *shuffle* in referring to the offensive sets he was implementing, but to me it looked like it was a way to tempt the odds. He was walking the players through their routes and describing how the ball would be passed here and there while player A screened for player B, and meanwhile C, D, and E were executing their moves. Whether the Anglers could ever successfully make so many passes without throwing the ball away or getting hopelessly perplexed was something I seriously questioned.

All the players acted confused. Crosse and his group were so new to organized basketball that I didn't wonder at their foul-ups. On the other hand, several of the others gave me the impression that they were purposely performing as if they were in a fog. I concluded that they had it in mind to drive Coach Levitson crazy with their ineptitude at carrying out his fresh plans, and thereby to force him to go back to the offense they knew so well. He would say "left" and they'd go right. He'd call for a pass, and someone would dribble instead. The Coach outlasted them though. His patience was infinite; his explanations of how it should have been done were calmly put. He showed no sign of backing off from his plan. Then I saw that Crosse, Lipscomb, Holeman, and Montler were catching on. Coach would yell, "That's the way, Montler!" and similar things to the others of the foursome, and this put the nine holdovers in a difficult position. If they continued their bumbling way, they just might be considered mentally slow in comparison to the new guys, something they couldn't afford, since their physical slowness was already a well established fact. There was general improvement as time went by, and an hour later Coach pronounced himself satisfied. The team was told to shoot its free throws again, and the practice ended shortly thereafter. There wasn't any locker room post-mortem following that practice, as there had been the day before. Five or six of the veterans left without even taking a shower, and the rest got out in a hurry. Jesse Crosse was the last one to leave that day, and I had a chance to talk to him for what amounted to the first time since he joined the team.

"You're looking pretty good out there, Crosse."

"Thanks, I haven't had a chance to thank you for what you did for us. John said you got us the tryout. I expect that your friends are angry or upset with you for doing that. I believe they'll forgive you before too long. We're going to have a good team."

I was surprised by his response to my conventional comments about his play. He was, in only one paragraph, appreciative of my efforts, perceptive regarding my standing with my friends, philosophical about my return to their good graces, and confident concerning the team's success. To tell the truth, I hadn't expected much more from him than a shy thank-you. What he said, and how he said it, gave me a strong feeling that there was a lot more to him than met the eye.

CHAPTER EIGHT

Our season was to begin in the first week of November. All the other schools in our league had football teams, and their basketball squads didn't begin to play until that fall ritual had come to a close, about the middle of the month. You might think that Jewelton held an advantage with that two-week head start, but the truth is that we typically had three, four, and once, I remember, even five losses before our league competitors ever played their first game. So it was common for the Anglers to have proved themselves to be the league's doormat before any conference games ever took place. In addition, the league's basketball teams all started practice at the same time we did, so we had no edge there either.

One thing I was absolutely sure about: No Angler team in my memory could compare to the one of 1960-61 in terms of its physical conditioning. Coach Levitson spent at least as much time running the players as he did trying to teach them the ins and outs of his new offense. For the next three weeks they ran more and more sprints; they ran laps outside the gymnasium; they even ran 10 miles one day, to and from Lake Tiberias. Coach sent me out, driving his car, to the lake in advance of the players' arrival, and I was to give each player a red rubber stamp mark on his hand to prove that he had been there. I recall that Jesse Crosse and Si Montler showed up first, and that they were amused by the stamp mark, which declared that they were "Property of Jewelton Athletic Department."

Crosse looked wryly at what I had stamped on his hand and said to me with a tone of feigned accusation, "I thought Mr. Lincoln put an end to such things." I didn't get it, so he expanded on the cryptic remark. "You remember the Emancipation Proclamation, don't you, Doc?" I then realized that he was referring to slavery, the first time I heard him comment on his blackness. The issue had not been ignored by others on the team, however. It was impossible to deny that Jesse's race was on the minds of some of the players. His comrades from the start, Lipscomb, Holeman, and Montler, were totally accepting of him; his color played no part in their relationship with him. I recall that Tradeau reported in rather scandalized tones that Jesse's three friends were frequently seen at his house and may even have had dinner with Jesse and his mother! Other players were less obvious about his race, although I heard the Alpheson brothers and Tradeau using the word "nigger" in a joking way after practice one day. Whether they were referring to Jesse or not, I never knew. The phrase I heard most often used to describe Jesse was "colored boy." And it was invariably used by most of the players who were not his friends. It was as if they refused to recognize him as having either a first or last name. Only Pete and Andy Barjon used the word "Negro," and they seldom employed that; to them he had become just "Crosse." I wasn't sure if Jesse's skin was much of a problem for him, but I could tell it was a problem for some of his teammates.

The 10-mile run and other strenuous demands of Coach Levitson began to take a back seat to running plays as our opening game with Cemaria drew closer. Cemaria was a little town that had no football team either, and we would face its team twice before our regular league play began. The first game was to be at Cemaria's gym, the second at ours. Cemaria was in a different league from us, and it was a 75-mile trip there, but both teams wanted early season contests, so the games were held every year. Bad blood existed between the two schools, apparently having to do with a fight that took place during a game at their gym several years before. Each side blamed the other, and the game had been called off by the officials, so explosive was the situation. The claim was heard in Jewelton that the night of the fight students and adults in Cemaria had thrown rocks at the Jewelton players' bus as it drove out of town, though I had also heard that story disputed by a man who said he was at the game. Coach Levitson never referred to Cemaria by name, talking instead about "our first opponent." But a few of our players were eager to stir up resentful feelings against the Travelers, as they were known.

Coach Levitson had been slowly imprinting the offensive maneuvers into the minds of the players. He had been taking them through what I would call "dry runs," since they didn't have any opposition while they practiced their moves and made their passes. There was still grumbling about his new schemes, as I could readily tell from the griping I heard after various practices. "We'll never be able to do it," and "It's too complicated," and "Nobody plays that way," were typical of the complaints. With only five practice days remaining before we journeyed to the home of the Travelers, I was beginning to think that perhaps the objectors were right. We had no idea how the new offense was going to work against an opponent, since we hadn't even tried it against ourselves.

There were only a handful of practice sessions left; the offense was an unknown quantity; some resentment still remained against the newcomers; we had some below-the-surface racial problems, and yet Coach Levitson looked happy as that day's practice began! I hadn't seen him so elated since the day he introduced all the offensive changes. Something was brewing.

"Boys, I know this has been a time of adjustment for all of you. What I also think I know is that some of you are not too happy with the alterations I've made." There were some affirmative glances exchanged when he said that. "So, I've decided to let this thing be worked out once and for all. First, I'd like to find out whether this unhappiness with the new offense is real or not." When he said this, and then said no more, the silence that followed was nerve-racking. He looked from player to player, but limited his gaze to the nine. They said nothing. So he took the bull by the horns. "Pete, tell me, do you approve of the new plays?" Pete was embarrassed, as if coach had picked him out as a leader of the discontent, which in fact he was not. What I had heard him say had been cautious with reference to the innovations. I believe he chose Pete because he knew that Pete would at least confess to being doubtful—which he did.

"Oh, I don't know, Coach, they're OK, I guess. I just wish we could find out if they work when somebody's trying to stop us, that's all." Pete's comments were probably about the mildest that any veteran Angler would have made if the truth were being told. Several of the others were much more vehement in the privacy of the dressing room. Coach Levitson smiled and said, "Let's just treat that as the tip of the iceberg, so to speak. I thank you for your observations, Pete, and I think the time has come to find out whether what we've been doing is any good or not. Let's just assume, for the sake of argument, that all of the players from last year's team have some doubts. Would that be a fair assumption? Would any of you other eight boys want to correct that?" Their silence was their assent. He continued, "I think I owe it to you to provide you with the offensive patterns that will bring out your talents." He said this with no sarcasm or irony. He was sincere. "I want to make a deal with you. Today we're going to have a game. You boys who know the offensive plays from last year are going to play against the boys who know only this year's plays. It will be a real game. I've asked Mr. Howard, who you know is a certified official, to referee." As if on cue, Tom Howard, who was a full-time pharmacist and a part-time official, came walking out of Coach's office wearing the traditional black and white shirt, black pants, and black shoes. There was amazement all around. There was to be even more. Coach Levitson announced, "Boys, I think we should settle this matter about the offense once and for all. We will run, for the rest of this year, the offense of the winning team."

First there was a gasp or two, and then much exultation from the group of nine. The Coach was going to let the game decide the issue! All they had to do was beat the newcomers, and all would be back to normal. It was the opportunity to get rid of all that had been in their craws since the first day of practice. They wouldn't squander the chance to put that all behind them. Coach had a couple of other announcements to make: "Luke is going to operate the scoreboard and keep track of fouls and so on. You nine will have to decide among yourselves who's going to substitute, and when. Is that all right?" They indicated that it was fine with them. The only problem with the arrangement eventually occurred to Johnny.

"Coach, they've only got four guys. We can't run our plays if we have just four, and they can't either. What are they going to do for a fifth man?" For a brief, anxious moment I feared that this was to be my debut in practice. I had hung around practice too much. Coach was going to make me play in this showdown! Maybe I deserved it. Then I realized that he'd already said I was to be the scorekeeper. It was impossible to play and keep score at the same time. He looked straight into Johnny's eyes and softly said, "I thought I'd be their fifth man, if nobody has any objections."

They were too surprised to object, and they probably wouldn't have, anyway. Coach was over 50, and while it was true that he had worked out with the team in past years when there was a player shortage, he hadn't spent a minute practicing the current year. They nodded their agreement to his proposal, and the two sides were set.

Coach Levitson, who was about six feet tall, towered over what were now his teammates. He huddled with them by one bench, and the nine seemed to think they should do the same sort of thing. Coach and his foursome shortly broke their huddle, but the nine stayed put, and I could hear them disagreeing about who would get to start. Finally they decided that the five seniors should have the honor, with Matt Tachsman, the younger Barjon, Wirges, and Alpheson brothers being the substitutes.

Mr. Howard brought the ball to midcourt for the opening tip-off. I hastily plugged in the clock and found that in front of me on the table was an official scorebook. I thought I'd have to delay the start of the game to write in all the players' names, but when I opened the book, I found that the names of the two teams were already there, neatly written in ink from what I recognized as Coach Levitson's fountain pen. We were ready to go.

Coach Levitson was going to jump against Pete, who had a height advantage of about two inches. Coach Levitson's team looked grim and nervous. They understood the significance of what was about to happen. If Pete and his team prevailed, the four would be out in the cold. They would spend the rest of the season trying to learn the old offense, and would be so handicapped by being behind the others that they would get playing time in the junior-varsity games only. There was little chance that they would ever make any important contribution.

Pete easily won the tip, not only due to his height advantage, but also to an ability to leap which four weeks of rugged conditioning had produced. Johnny dribbled the ball toward the basket and began to put into play the old Angler attack. One or two passes later, Tom Dubius surprised all by taking and making a long shot from the corner. "They're really confident," I thought. Ordinarily Dubius would be the last one I would have expected to shoot, so limited was he in that talent. The Levitson-led crew, following the principles they had learned over the past weeks, took the ball out of bounds and flew down the court. I was surprised at how fast Coach was. It was clear that Pete and his mates were anticipating that charge, however, and they were prepared to defend. To get a fast break after the other team's score is very difficult because of the time lost in-bounding the ball. So it was to be expected that Levitson's team would have to work the ball. I was in a state of high anticipation to see how the pass-pass offense which Coach had installed would work. Jesse fired a pass to Lipscomb, who in turn threw one to the Coach. In violation of all that he had taught over the past weeks, he shot! No waiting for the easy basket, as he had instructed. No wearing down the desire of the other team to play defense, as he had counseled. He threw up a wild shot that wasn't even close. In an effort to make immediate amends, Coach charged the backboard for a rebound and fouled Pete. He immediately asked Mr. Howard for a time out. The gym was so quiet that I could overhear the huddle talk of both teams, placed as I was in between them at the scorer's table.

Coach was apologizing to his team. I heard him say, "I lost my head, and I'm sorry." It was very surprising to hear the Coach blaming himself, but it was astonishing to hear the reply of Jesse Crosse: "That's all right, Coach, we'll get it back." So matter-of-fact, so forgiving, so crazy a thing to say to the head coach! Meanwhile, to my right, I also overheard a heated discussion of whether it was time to substitute or not. The bench players wanted into the fray, and the others were trying to convince them that there was no call to substitute yet, since the game was less than two minutes old.

Mr. Howard's whistle brought the players back and play resumed. Not much happened for the next 30 seconds, but then Montler intercepted a pass, and the fast break was on. He zinged the ball to Crosse, who was dashing down the floor with Coach Levitson on his left and Lipscomb on his right. Only Tradeau, who had thrown the failed pass, was between the three offensive players and the goal. Tradeau knew he was a dead duck. He stood no chance against the three of them. He resorted to a low tactic. I could see it coming. He pulled up in the center of the court and was preparing to trip Crosse. As he stuck out his leg far enough to be effective, he closed his eyes in preparation for the collision that was about to occur. Crosse jumped at the last possible second to avoid the contact, and while in mid-air and moving rapidly toward the sideline he lobbed a gentle pass to the Coach, who dropped it in. Tradeau was mystified as he opened his eyes. Jesse Crosse, who had landed at least five feet to the right of where Tradeau was expecting him to be, was already backpedaling toward the other goal and yelling to Coach, "Good shot!"

What Tradeau found incomprehensible, his teammates found funny. The raucous laughter, at what had begun as a cheap attempt to knock down another player but had resulted in a bamboozled defenseman, was merciless. The humiliated Tradeau had to retrieve the ball from under the goal to throw it in, and he looked enraged. And so the contest continued.

The shooting of the veterans returned to what I viewed as "normal" after Dubius made his first basket, which is to say that they made only a modest percentage of their shots, and the first quarter ended with the score 10-10. The two teams looked evenly matched at that point, although Coach Levitson had lost the spring in his step and spent most of the time between quarters trying to replenish his oxygen supply rather than giving instructions. But Jesse was not at a loss for breath or words. I noted that he was instructing the others, including the Coach, on what they could do that quarter to improve. Coach was breathing hard, but he was listening.

The second quarter began as the first, with Pete's side getting the first possession. Crosse promptly stole the ball from Jim Wirges, who, along with the other three subs, had gotten into the game. Jesse went into his overdrive gear after swiping the ball, but slowed enough to toss it to Holeman for another layup and the first lead for the team I had considered the underdog. Again Jim brought the ball up against Crosse, and once more he lost it. It was plain that Crosse was playing with a ferocity which he did not exhibit at first. He was hounding the dribbler, darting back and forth at the ball in a way that had Jim totally intimidated. After his second steal, Jesse had to wait for his teammates to catch up to him, and the new offense went into its complex array of passes and screens and cuts for the goal. For the first time I saw what the possibilities were. Over and over the Levitson five executed their patterns without a flaw. The defenders, who presumably knew everything that was going on, were starting to look disorganized. On at least three occasions the offensive team had an easy chance to try a shot from close range, but they passed each one up. Once, right in front of the goal, Coach Levitson had a near layup and turned it down. He flipped the ball out to Lipscomb, and the intricate maze of patterns began all over again. The Coach's team must have kept the ball for more than two minutes before a brilliant pass from Crosse eventually found Lipscomb so alone at the basket that he was almost obliged in conscience to shoot and thereby have mercy on the weary defenders. The team of nine called for time.

There wasn't much conversation in either huddle, except for the insistence in one that the four substitutes come out of the game. The four fresh players made no difference. The hustling, torrid defense of Coach's team, in combination with occasional fast breaks and successfully completing their plays, left the score 28-14 at halftime. The only problem that I could see for the former underdogs was whether Coach Levitson could hold up. He looked drained, and the five minutes between halves didn't give him nearly enough time to recuperate.

The third quarter began with a basket by Pete. It was the last one he or his team got. The Levitson crew was in full cry throughout the rest of the quarter. Crosse was everywhere. Lipscomb, Montler, and Holeman were almost as ubiquitous. Coach was hanging on gamely. The fast break and the plays intended to complement it worked almost to perfection. Time after time Crosse made passes to open teammates who had shots so easy that I could have made them. I admit that I couldn't have moved fast enough to get into position to make them, but the shots themselves were a cinch. The score at the end of the third period was 40-16. Coach's team, by my count, had missed only one shot, while the other side had made only one. The big question about the fourth quarter, whether Coach Levitson would survive it, never had to be addressed. From the group of nine fatigued ballplayers I heard tired but angry voices that they were trying with limited success to muffle. Pete's powerful vocal cords eventually prevailed, and then he walked alone to the Coach, whose hands on knees and heaving chest were a barometer of his condition.

"Coach," Pete said quietly, "We've had enough. You win. Everything."

Coach Levitson could only bob his head up and down to acknowledge the concession. He, and the four, had triumphed. It was true that although the victory went to the five of them, Jesse Crosse had dominated all that had happened on the court that afternoon. When I looked closely at the scorebook, however, I saw that he had not scored a point.

CHAPTER NINE

I looked at the scoreboard one last time to confirm that the margin of victory was 24 points; then I hurriedly unplugged the clock and took the basketballs and the scorebook to Coach's office. He was there, covered with sweat and still not breathing normally. He weakly raised his hand to me in greeting as I entered, and he managed a faint smile. "Luke, I think you must have made a mistake with that clock. High school quarters are supposed to last only eight minutes, and I'm sure you must have let them go for 16." His facetious explanation for his exhaustion wasn't necessary. I was proud of the stamina he had shown, even if it was for only 24 minutes of playing time. His hair was soaked and matted, and his shirt was dripping, but I didn't know when he ever looked better. Somehow the game had evoked youthfulness in him; I guess he reminded me of the sweat-soaked players who were more than 30 years younger. He rose from his swivel chair with obvious difficulty, and said, "I think it's time I had a talk with the boys."

It was unknown for Coach Levitson to visit the players' dressing room after practice. His pattern in coming there was restricted to his chalk talks before a game. I knew that the sight of him in their midst would be another shock to the players on this already very shocking day. I hesitated, not knowing whether I should go, too. He had taken a few painful steps out of his office when he sensed that I wasn't following him. He turned and ordered, "Come along, Luke; we're all in this together."

As I pushed open the swinging door to the locker room, I heard none of the usual chatter and horseplay that followed a practice. The sound, or lack of it, was odd, but the sight inside was odder. All the players were just sitting. None had headed for the showers; they hadn't even removed their practice gear. They were waiting for something to happen or to be said. Did they sense that the Coach was coming? Maybe I was wrong in thinking that they would be surprised to see him. They looked as if they expected it.

He didn't explain his unusual arrival. He cleared his throat and began: "Boys, this has been a difficult time in many ways. I don't need to list them; you know them. I want you to consider one thing, and then I'm going to leave. We are basically a team. Not 13 individuals. This team has promise. Very few teams, in my time as coach, have had such promise. I think we're going to be better this year than anyone outside, and maybe even inside, this locker room would expect. You each have an opportunity to be part of something that people will remember for a long time. This isn't some phony lecture to boost your morale. I believe this."

Coach's sincerity was evident. Whether his predictions were accurate was another thing entirely. The players were responding still as two groups. Jesse and his friends were soaking up his words, intently eyeing him. The nine were looking at the floor or the ceiling, unwilling to meet the look of one so earnestly addressing them. Coach Levitson detected the indifference to, or rejection of what he was saying. It lit a spark in him, or, more accurately, set off an explosion in him. He paused for a moment and then shouted in a way that bounced off the walls of that confined space and banged into every person there. "Damn it! Would you boys quit being so selfish for a minute?"

I had always admired Coach's selective use of his *damns* and *hells*. They never failed to produce rapt attention. When an Angler heard one, he knew he'd better listen. Coach lowered his voice a few decibels, but he was still angry. This too was rare in him, and its effect was that all eyes were now on him. His voice shuddered as he attempted to keep his anger under some control. "I'm going to level with you. I don't like what I've seen from some of you. I'm going to name names, and you can take it or leave it. We had four new boys join this team this year, and you other boys have behaved badly toward them from the start. Frankly, I don't know how they have put up with your lack of civility. And if 'civility' is not clear to you, then maybe this will make it clearer—you have been narrow-minded and unfriendly and, worst of all, prejudiced."

Coach was tackling head-on the issue of Jesse Crosse's color. Some broke off eye contact when he said that, but the rising anger in his voice brought it back. "I'm ready today, this afternoon, to hear from anyone on this team who is convinced that he can't work with everyone else to make this the best team possible. I've watched you, hoping that you could work this out yourselves. I don't think you've done it."

The sight of Coach Levitson enraged was almost terrifying. His fierceness had not diminished for a second. Then he turned on Pete. "Barjon, you sort

of imagine yourself as a leader of this group, don't you?" I didn't expect Pete
to answer, and he didn't. But he didn't shy away from Coach's glare. He was
going to take whatever was about to come. "You don't have to say anything,
Barjon; we all know that you pride yourself on being the number-one man.
There is a certain justification in that too. You have, in some ways, earned that
place of respect on this team. So it's all the worse for you that you didn't step
in and put a halt to all the negative things that have been going on lately, isn't
it?" The question at the end was a threatening thing, because in the silence
that followed I knew that Coach was going to force Pete to answer. Pete knew
it too. I could see him trying to summon up his reply. Then he began to cry!
His words were interfered with by his emotions, but what he said was crystal:
"Yes, sir; I'm ashamed of myself for it."

That was all. That was enough. The aftermath was excruciating. Pete was
sobbing, and there was nothing else to be heard. Coach was not satisfied. Not
only had he cracked Pete for a second time, and even more profoundly than
at practice, but he wanted to confront us all it seemed. "Tradeau, you need
some attention from me too." Tradeau almost fell off the bench. He pulled in
his shoulders like a man about to be whipped. He looked at his feet and waited
for the punishment. Coach was unsparing of him. "No, I don't expect you to
look me in the eye. That would be too out of character for the way you've been
acting lately. I saw you try to trip Crosse. I've seen you muttering, and I've
sensed your resentment against him and the others. You see it slipping away,
don't you? Your senior year—a chance to get a lot of playing time—a chance
to be a big man on campus. How wrong you were! You would have been the
ninth man on a nine-man team. You could count on one hand the number of
minutes you would have gotten to play this year. Yet when I talked about two
teams playing equally, you couldn't see that I was offering you a chance to get
more playing time than you ever would have gotten under the old system. But
you were too ignorant to see that—or too self-centered."

I had never heard such an indictment from Coach Levitson. He was in
no mood to spare feelings or illusions. He was brutal, but he was right. His
two outbursts against Pete and Tradeau calmed him. He looked at the other
seven and simply said, "You have all failed in some ways in this, haven't you?"
Once again, the inquiry demanded a response. They meekly acknowledged
their guilt with barely audible words. The fire was burning low in Coach at
that point, but it wasn't out. I was last on his list. "Luke, what about you? You
watch after the bumps and bruises, but when something is seriously wrong
with the whole team, what do you do? Hide your head in the sand. If the
patient is going to get better, Doc, you can't ignore the illness." He had me

reeling. I knew he was right, but I wanted to plead my case. I wanted to say that I'd never said "nigger," that I'd never encouraged the resentment, but I realized that he wasn't accusing me of that. He said that I had stood by and watched as something evil spread, and had done nothing really to stop it. I had no defense against that charge.

He summed it all up. "Boys, some hard words have been said here today. I don't expect all of you to like them. I want you to decide before you leave today whether what you've heard has made you feel that you don't want to be part of this team anymore. I will understand if you want to separate yourself from us as of today. So if you feel that way, I want you to come to my office and tell me so—today!" His emphasis on the last word startled us once more. He was drawing the line unmistakably. "If you decide to stay with us, let it be understood it is only because you can see that the welfare of the team is the most important thing in your mind. I want no more jealousy, no more dissension, no more division. I want to coach two units, but only one team. I hope you understand this clearly. I'll be in my office." With that, he left.

It was as if the air had been sucked out of that room. For a few seconds no one made a move. No one spoke. The first voice was that of Jesse Crosse. It was low, but firm, and I looked at him as he stood up. A 10th grader, the smallest of us all, was daring to add to the welter of things that had been said. I couldn't imagine what he intended to say.

"Guys, we can have a great team, but only if everybody stays." That was all he said, and no one added anything to it. In silence, they began to drift to the showers. I was the last to leave, as usual, and I watched intently as all departed. None went in the direction of Coach's office.

CHAPTER TEN

Memory is hard to explain. I've never been able to determine how my own memories of that year have fallen into two parts. The recollection of our basketball season is marked by a dividing line created by Coach Levitson's appearance in the locker room. Up to that time, I remember most vividly what people said. I do have a few clear visual memories, like Jesse Crosse's first phenomenal pass, but I'm surprised and unable to explain why there are few other images of that sort. But beginning with the next day's practice, my mind latched on to sights as well as sounds—perhaps an equal number of both. I mention this because it's noticeable to me and may be to you. Of course I had my journal to remind me of events, but the details have come from my memory, not pieces of paper.

Why my mind began to hang on to so many of the things I saw, in addition to what I heard, I don't know. Until Coach's powerful intervention into the problems of the team, I was doubtful about lots of things—whether Crosse and the others would be accepted, whether Coach's new plans would work, what kind of success we would have. But after he forced us to face the issues that had to be resolved, I began to feel that stability was possible. The team might be able to come together and function as one. With doubt removed or greatly diminished, I think I started to believe what he had said: that this could be a team that people would remember—and I would, too.

Everyone practiced the next day. All had decided to stay on the team. Not much conversation was evident before practice, but I heard Tradeau greet Jesse for the first time. Tradeau's head ducked as he said, "Hey, Crosse," almost as if he did not want to take credit or responsibility for what he had done. Jesse's broad smile and returned greeting indicated that he was happy with the way things were working out. As I looked at him tying his shoe laces, I groped for some explanation for his basketball talent. He still looked like "five-three and a hundred-and-three" to me. His practice shorts were our smallest size, yet they hung long and droopy on him, almost half-way down his thighs. His scooped neck jersey, also the smallest in our inventory, gaped at the arms and, when not tucked into his shorts, hung so low that it virtually made the shorts disappear. I knew that our game uniforms would fit him no better, and I feared that he would be a ridiculous sight if his number ended up tucked into his pants. The sight of him just didn't coincide with what I knew he was able to do on the court. The fans, theirs and ours, who probably would be amused by the sight of him, were in for an awakening.

All the remaining practices leading up to our first game were exciting— especially the last. Coach Levitson, arms waving and whistle blowing, was communicating a sense of urgency to the team. Coach was using several combinations to try to determine the mix that he wanted. He was working hard to implement his two-team theory, but time was running out on him. Then, the day before the game he told us that he had it. First of all, he told a glum Tachsman and Tradeau and Jim Wirges that they were to be the substitutes for each unit. He was very kind about the assignments, telling them that they would surely see action, and that their game and practice performances could elevate them onto the starting roles of their respective fives. The two teams were known as "Red" and "White," a practical use of the school colors. Coach Levitson insisted that there was no "first" team in the usual sense. One group would undoubtedly start the game, but the two fives would alternate quarters, so the team that didn't play until the second quarter would have the vital function of playing the last quarter, when so many crucial events related to winning or losing took place. He announced that Jesse Crosse and Si Montler would be point men for the Red and the White, that Holeman and Lipscomb would be split, too. Pete and Tom, as the tallest of the Anglers would be the centers, and all the rest would divide time at forward.

Coach peered up from his clipboard after reading out the assignments, as if checking for signs of the old disagreement or dissatisfaction. His pleased look apparently meant that he found none. Practice that final day returned to the dry-run routines, with each five carrying out its assignments with no one to oppose them. In what I thought was a very short time, Coach trilled his whistle and ordered that free throws be shot. The season was upon us. All that remained was for me to hand out the equipment that each player would need for the season. Each got a fire-engine red traveling bag with straps, with *Jewelton* written in white thereon, to use to transport either the white jersey, for home games, with *Anglers* and a number broadly written in red on the chest and shorts of the same color, or a red top and bottom with the same markings (but in white) for the away games. Though the veterans were anticipating them, the new, white Converse All-Stars that I gave to each player was an obviously pleasant shock to Jesse and the other three newcomers. A week before I had checked the sizes of the four pairs of threadbare (and rubberbare as well) high-tops of the newcomers when they had gone to shower after practice. Eight eyes glowed as I handed out the new shoes, along with two new pairs of socks for each.

"How did you know what size to get?" Si asked in wonder.

"Doc knows all," Pete explained. I grinned, more than ready for our first game.

★★★★★

The bus ride to Cemaria always seemed to take more time than a 75-mile trip should. I've mentioned Coach's turtle-like approach to driving. Add to that my eagerness to see the Anglers try out all that was new, and you can understand why I felt the drive go by as if in slow motion. The players were very loose and happy. Johnny sat with Jesse and they chattered a lot about what it was like to play at Cemaria, with Johnny describing the rabid fans and the peculiarities of their gym as compared with ours. A couple of times the players tried to stir up some of the old animosity against the Travelers, but it came to a halt when Pete told Jimmy Alpheson that we didn't need to be digging up some ancient grudge.

As the yellow school bus eased along the four-lane highway, with cars constantly overtaking us and passing in a flash, I wondered whether the newly discovered spirit would last long if Cemaria handed us our heads on a platter. A resounding defeat, or even a close loss, might start to pull apart the team's new cohesiveness. I couldn't help but be skeptical of how deep the healing process had gone. What if the new guys freeze up? What if the new offense doesn't work against the Travelers? Would things return to their original, sorry state? As these doubts began to invade, I suddenly wasn't so keen on getting to Cemaria. I just wanted the harmony and optimism to last and last, untested by the reality of the game.

"Cemaria—Population 3,257—Home of the Fried Dill Pickle" was the blue and white sign at its outskirts. I thought of my initial reaction to that sign as we drove by it on my first out-of-town basketball trip three years before. Why didn't it say, "Welcome?" And what was a fried dill pickle? I have since found out that a local café, which paid for the sign, was advertizing one of its menu items as well as the presence of the town. The reason for the lack of a friendly greeting I never discovered. As I looked out the window of the bus, I could tell by familiar landmarks that Coach Levitson was guiding us with a sure hand to the gymnasium he had visited so many times before. I was thinking about estimating the number of miles he had driven to and from that town on basketball trips when I noticed that my breath fogged the window. I had been unaware that the night had grown so much colder. The lights of the squat Cemaria gym twinkled in the distance, and I experienced a feeling of happiness. This was really it! The sudden snap in temperature, the predictable slow progress of the bus, the sight of the place where our boys would confront their first foe—all these things combined to lift my spirits. Even though I wasn't much good at it, I really loved basketball!

A hush fell over the team as we drove up to the gym. We could hear a drum pounding and hands clapping. People who had left Jewelton to see the game, mostly parents and friends, were pulling up in the dusty lot next to the gym, too. They hailed us with good wishes as we got off, and we headed for the locker room with hopes high.

There was no junior varsity game scheduled for that night, so everyone had to dress right away. Ordinarily, those who were playing in the varsity game would wait until the half of the first game before putting on their uniforms. The tension in the locker room was stimulating, even to one who was not scheduled to play. I could feel a certain amount of tightness in my stomach, and I knew that it was only a part of what the players were going through. The locker room at other schools always made me uncomfortable. I'd been to Cemaria three times, but that made the place no less alien. It was especially unpleasant this night. Dozens of paper towels were scattered on the floor, and several were still damp, as though someone had just remembered to come in and litter, intentionally giving the room an inhospitable air. On a portable blackboard supposedly left there for the convenience of our coach, there was scrawled, "Something smells fishie." I contrasted the atmosphere with the pains to which Coach Levitson (and I as his emissary of good will) went to make our visitors' dressing room pleasant.

He always made sure I checked the room for cleanliness before the other team arrived, washed the blackboard and supplied it with unused chalk and a clean eraser. For my first two years as a manager, he told me to provide the visitors with 20 freshly laundered towels, a practice he ordered stopped when many of them were stolen and others were found clogging up the drain in the shower room. To make the visitors' locker room agreeable was obviously not important to the Cemaria coach. What was worse, the room was powerful in its odor of unflushed and uncleaned toilets, and I wondered what else could possibly have been done to make us feel less welcome.

When the lights went out while the players were getting dressed, I acknowledged that more could be done. Coach immediately sent me to find Cemaria's coach to alert him to our predicament. As I left the locker room and entered the gym, I saw four large, unfriendly looking boys standing only a few feet away from what I would discover was the fuse box. Their coach, Farris by name, acted as if I had turned out the lights myself. He was acutely irritated that I knocked on his dressing room and asked to see him. Farris, who huffily stormed to the fuse box and flipped a switch, paid no attention to the now grinning group which I knew had brought on the darkness. I wasn't as happy about the game as I had been 15 minutes before.

After all were dressed, Coach instructed the players about their warm-up drills, and they somberly took to the floor. They too were in a less exuberant mood. I made a mental note to ask Coach Levitson if there wouldn't be some advantage for us to make our visitors' locker room as cruddy as possible. And a well-timed blackout would apparently help to diminish the other team's enthusiasm, too. The gymnasium was everywhere plastered with blue and white, and an unusually large number of signs mocking us. Rather than messages of support for the Travelers, these were the stereotypical negative comments about Jewelton. Maybe Cemaria was just an unfriendly town— maybe that's why it never crossed anyone's mind to bid a visitor welcome.

The warm-up was over, and I noticed that the supporters from Cemaria had spotted Jesse and were preparing to make him the target of their derision, should he ever set foot on the court as a player. His size, his color, his ill-fitting uniform, all conspired to accentuate his otherness. I could see them pointing and laughing at him, and they were bending low and bouncing around in the stands in imitation of his lack of height. Part of the suspense during the locker room talk by Coach Levitson prior to the game was irrelevant to the game itself. Would the lights stay on? Could we survive the odor of the place? Perhaps these factors accounted for the terseness of the words from Coach. He reminded the players of how hard they had prepared, and asked them to have confidence in their offense. "It will work, I promise you. Just don't lose faith, even if it doesn't work perfectly from the start. Let's go out and have some fun!"

Fun was the last thing on the minds of the folks from Cemaria. Their players were menacing and acted reluctant even to shake hands with our players as the tip-off approached. The fans were rowdy and screamed more at our players than for their own. The White team with Si Montler at the point guard position opened up the game for the Anglers, and I was thrilled to see Tom outjump their taller center. Si was iceberg cool as he set the first offensive play in motion. My heart leaped as I saw the Anglers running their routes, making crisp passes, and working as smoothly as I'd ever seen them do at practice. We passed and passed some more. It was clear that the Travelers weren't crazy about the time they were having to spend on defense, and the fans quickly assaulted our guys with non-stop booing for what they thought was some sort of stall game. We weren't stalling; we were trying to wear them down until one defensive man made a mistake. And then one did. Tom was underneath the basket wide open. Si spotted him and fired the ball. It was too far in front of Tom and went off his fingers out of bounds. The hooting from the stands was especially painful. We had been so close to making it work to perfection! I could see the deflated looks on our players' faces as they hurried back to the defense. On the one hand, they must have recognized how well they had worked the ball, and how close they had come to an uncontested shot. On the other, their precision and patience had availed them nothing, and that was made even worse when a Traveler hit a long shot not five seconds after the ball had crossed the center stripe.

The first failure to score took the wind out of the White's sails. They played hard but tentatively for the rest of the quarter, and we trailed after eight minutes, 14-6. As the Red team checked in with the scorer to start the second quarter, I could see the wolves in the Cemaria stands getting ready for Jesse. They were nudging each other and pointing out the diminutive black player; he was a marked man. Cemaria had no black players, and the sight of Jesse's skin in relation to all the rest was indeed a matter of sharpest contrast. The Cemarian crowd quickly took up someone's dub of him as "Pee Wee," and they were having a good time of it at his expense. Jesse looked nervous for the first time since I had known him. He was rubbing his hands, actually almost wringing them. I felt sorry for him, standing by himself at the free-throw line, to defend our goal against any attempt to score rapidly on the tip-off. No Traveler stood by him, and he was directly in front of the loudest of the spectators. Mercifully the referee stepped in and tossed the ball for the tip. Pete jumped even higher against the Traveler center than Tom had, and he soundly batted the ball back to Jesse.

The fans created a hostile crescendo as Jesse dribbled the ball up the court. Now that he had the ball, his nervousness had disappeared. He directed the play of the Anglers, and, as on our first possession, our team was methodically running its offense. The crowd became enraged by the deliberateness of our play, and they set about doing all they could to disrupt it. I began to worry that the turmoil would take its toll. Another bad pass and we might be cooked for the night. All was operating smoothly except for the fact that no one was getting open. The Travelers were playing rugged defense, sensing that to turn back this play might have the same effect on the Reds as it had had on the Whites. Then, under the basket, with the ball, and then with two points, was Jimmy Alpheson. Jesse had done it again! Behind the back went his pass. He never looked at Jimmy. One second it was in Jesse's hands, then another and it was in Jimmy's. There were 10 of us on the bench, and then there were 10 of us off the bench screaming our approval. The crowd disappeared momentarily. They were dazed by what they had seen.

As Cemaria began its attack, the fans began to buzz, as if trying to assure each other that what had happened had really happened. They had little time to adjust though. Jesse sneaked up behind their center and wrenched the ball away from him. He and the other Anglers stormed to the other end. But he stopped. I didn't know what to think as he lofted the ball far down the court to what looked like nobody in particular. Then I saw, finally, what Jesse had seen from the start: Pete had an angle on everybody to the goal, and he sped to the rainbow lob without breaking stride and made the shot unimpeded. It was 14-10, and we were coming back!

About 30 seconds later when Jesse sprained his wrist diving for a ball, I was happy. Not happy then, but happy to be told later that it was not broken. At first I was certain that it was fractured, so limply did it hang. The swelling was almost immediate. What pleased me most about an incident that otherwise made me sick was that the people of Cemaria did an about-face. They cheered for Jesse as he was helped from the floor by Coach Levitson and me. There was no scorn in their voices, nor were they acting as if they were glad to see him go. They knew that he had done, in little more than three minutes, some special things on the court. Not only did the fans applaud his efforts, but a man came from the bleachers and identified himself as a doctor. He volunteered to take Jesse to his office for X-rays. Coach sent me along, and I gladly confess that the earnest doctor, who drove us to his nearby office, found no break and merely wrapped Jesse's wrist, and the fan reaction to Jesse's injury, made me do some revision in my opinion of the people of Cemaria.

When we got back from the doctor's office, we discovered the team in the locker room, just about ready for the long ride home after a 52-46 loss. Pete looked at Jesse as he came in the door, inquired about his wrist, and said, "We'd have won if you hadn't gotten hurt."

CHAPTER ELEVEN

The two most encouraging things about the loss to Cemaria were that Jesse was recovering speedily and the team had continued to function as a team throughout the whole game. Johnny was telling me about the play of the Anglers after Jesse had to leave: "We could see that his way of doing it, constantly looking for the guy with the better shot, worked!" Johnny was about as happy as you could expect a player to be in the wake of a defeat. He had been converted to the Levitson vision of how basketball should be played, and had adopted the Crosse way of accomplishing it. I was incredulous to hear that our high scorers for the game had been Tom and Pete. Pete's 12 points didn't surprise me, but Tom's total did. I asked Johnny how Tom, who was one of the weakest players the year before, was able to get a dozen. He smiled in a way that indicated he understood my amazement. "We just kept working the ball until somebody got open, and Tom just turned out to be the one who was in the clear. I think Tom had as hard a time as anybody believing that Coach's plan would work. Maybe he was the last to be convinced. But he's not stupid. After he saw Jesse and the others who play like him getting the ball to guys right under the basket, he finally became a believer. I'm pretty sure the fact that he tied Pete for high point man had a lot to do with it, too. Anyway, he's crazy about the new offense now, and can't wait to play Cemaria again on Friday."

We had the return game with Cemaria and one with Bethany before we were to start league play. If we could win one of those two, we might not look like sitting ducks to the rest of the league. By Thursday's practice it was clear that Jesse was back to normal. For some reason I began to search my memory as I watched Thursday's spirited practice. The question had occurred to me whether I had ever seen Jesse shoot the ball except in warm-ups.

For so many players, the shot is the seductive element in basketball. Even the worst players can heave the ball up enough times that the law of averages seems to ultimately reward them. To score is to stand out. For that moment, when the ball nestles in the net, every player knows all eyes are on him. To make the shot is to guarantee that one is admired and cheered, if only briefly. I couldn't figure why that element of the game had no attraction for Jesse. His shooting in warm-ups was excellent, but it was limited mostly to layups. I would have been tempted to say that he knew that those short ones were the only shots he could make, but even so, he had ample opportunities to take them in scrimmage at practice, but he always passed to someone else. I knew, however, that Jesse wasn't limited to making the close-in shots. I had watched him shoot many a free throw at the end of every practice, and he could be counted on to sink eight out of every 10 he tried. What was his reason for shooting only when it didn't count?

At that last practice before the second Cemaria game, I eased up next to Coach Levitson to try to discuss with him the phenomenon of Jesse's lack of interest in scoring. I employed the direct approach rather than beat about the bush. "Coach, how come Crosse never shoots?"

He looked a little surprised at my abruptness, but then laughed and replied, "When did you notice that?" I knew then that I had been right in thinking that Jesse had been abstaining from shooting.

"It just occurred to me as I was watching the layups. He hasn't taken a shot yet in practice, has he? And I know he didn't shoot against Cemaria. I noticed it first when I looked at the scorebook after that game at practice. He just ran circles around the other team, but I was surprised to see that he hadn't scored. How come? He can shoot, I've seen him hit his free throws, and he sure could have had a bunch of fast-break buckets. Has he got some sort of problem about shooting?"

Coach laughed heartily. I felt I had asked a perfectly reasonable question, and he was treating it as if it were absurd. "No, Doc, I'm sure he doesn't have a 'problem,' as you put it. He's just got a different way of playing basketball compared to most kids his age. His idea is to give the ball to the other guy. Never worry about your points; don't think about your average or getting your name in the paper. Just play for the team. He seems thoroughly committed to that. I've never seen a player who was so dedicated to doing everything he could to making his teammates look good. And you know better than anyone that he had that attitude before he ever came to our team. Where he got the idea, I don't know. But I could see it from the start, and that's why I decided to install the offense. Heck, I've wanted to run that type of offense for years, but I never had the players that could make it work. It took a certain kind of player to make it go; somebody who could make it click over and over in practice until the other kids would believe in it. There's a big difference between telling them that it will work, and having somebody like Crosse showing them it will."

I didn't expect my original question to turn up so much. Coach Levitson's recital of the benefits of a player like Jesse was accompanied by a glint in his eye, reminding me of those times in his English class when he would get really excited about the truth and beauty of a particular poem. I had seen that look of enchantment on his face before, but not in conjunction with basketball. He was plainly a happy man as we readied ourselves for the game with the Travelers.

★★★★★

The highlights of that second game are many. First, of all, we won 52-38. The low score by Cemaria was largely due to the fact that our guys made them play a lot of defense. I only wish I had a nickel for every pass we made. Si Montler did a fine job of leading the White unit, and Jesse was astonishing for the Red.

An "assist" in basketball is a little-known and less-appreciated aspect of the game except to the most ardent fan. When a player makes a pass that directly leads to a teammate's basket, he is given credit for an assist in the scoring of the two points. It's a way of recognizing the value of the well-timed, well-thrown pass. Jesse had 18 assists against Cemaria. His passes brought about 36 of our points. As manager, I kept statistics during the game: how many shots a player took and made, how many rebounds he got, and other elements that can be numbered. I had done this for more than three years for the Anglers, and I'm certain that no Jewelton player ever had as many as 10 assists in any game during my time of keeping track of such things. Jesse was so quick in his passing that twice he fired the ball to wide-open Anglers who were not expecting the passes, and the ball flashed right past them.

When Jesse entered the game with the rest of the Red crew to start the second quarter, a bizarre thing took place. He was the last of the five to go onto the floor, and our fans suddenly got very quiet. It was their first encounter with Jesse as a player, and they were silenced by the sight of him. You can imagine how he looked to them. With his jersey No. 5 stuffed partly down in his pants to the point that the number was almost not recognizable, he must have seemed like a refugee from a junior high game who had gotten misdirected into a contest for older, larger boys.

The muted response from our supporters was then countered by applause, which undoubtedly was for Jesse. It came from the handful of people

who were there to cheer for the Travelers! Remembering his performance of
a few nights before and seeing that he had recovered from his injury, they
warmly welcomed him back to the court. Jesse appeared embarrassed by their
approval, but he didn't ignore it. He turned slightly in their direction and
waved at them as he had to me at the end of a practice many weeks before.
He wasn't the kind to be ungrateful, even if it meant adding another element
of the unusual to an already strange situation. The fans in the bleachers who
were not from Cemaria were dumbfounded by the turn of events. Why would
the Travelers' fans be clapping for one of our players? The answer came as the
quarter progressed.

From its outset, Jesse was a dervish. His speed was too much for the
guards from Cemaria. He roared past them on fast breaks, hounded them
when they had the ball, and made, according to my record-keeping, six steals.
He evoked oohs and aahs from our backers with a variety of passes which
they didn't anticipate and could only appreciate in retrospect.

The play that symbolized for me the change that had come over the
team since Coach Levitson's chewing-out was Jesse's length-of-the-court toss
to Tradeau for our final two points. True to his word, Coach Levitson was
getting all the players some playing time, and Tradeau played much of the
fourth quarter, when it was becoming clear to the Jewelton crowd that we were
going to win. They roared their approval at every play which worked to our
advantage, and especially rewarded the substitutes when they did something
good. Tradeau's basket came with less than a minute to go, and he looked
thrilled as the sounds of support cascaded down on him after his basket. In
the din, I could see him mouth the words, "Good pass," to Jesse. Tradeau had
come a long way since the day he wanted to knock Jesse down at practice.

Cemaria tried a last, futile shot with about 30 seconds to go, and Jesse
disdained a final fast-break opportunity to avoid running up the score. Under
his command, the Anglers methodically passed the ball until time ran out,
and Jewelton had its first win. Our fans went into a frenzy when the red
numbers on the scoreboard showed 0:00 to play. They ran onto the court and
pounded the players on the back and acted as if we had won the league title,
instead of our first game of the year. Coach Levitson was the beneficiary of
many forms of congratulations, and his beaming face showed his joy. There
was an atmosphere in the gymnasium that made the three past years a gladly
forgotten memory. Long-time, long-suffering supporters of Jewelton teams
were celebrating something new and exciting.

I ran into Mr. and Mrs. Morgan, whose son had played six or seven years
before for the Anglers; they had remained faithful followers of our team long

after their boy had graduated. "Luke, I've never seen them play so well!" Mr. Morgan crowed. Since his devotion to the Anglers gave him a much lengthier exposure to Jewelton basketball than I had, I took his comment as being important. He and his wife had witnessed enough of the game in their many years as fans to make them knowledgeable observers whose opinions carried weight. "What'd you think, Mrs. Morgan?" I yelled above the pandemonium which still raged.

A tiny, white-haired, grandmotherly looking lady is not the image of a person who qualifies as a basketball sage, but I thought her analysis was absolutely correct: "That little Crosse boy makes all the difference, Luke. He's marvelous!" As I said goodbye to the happy pair and walked to the locker room, I realized that Jesse had finally scored. He made two points on two free-throw attempts. That wouldn't look like much in the box score, but his importance to our team's welfare was beyond dispute. How vital he was would not be clear to those who only read the newspaper accounts of our games. That is, not until our next one, scheduled for the gym at Bethany.

CHAPTER TWELVE

A school bus seems to be entirely made of metal when the temperature drops. Even the padded seats feel like cold steel if the thermometer has dipped as much as it did the night we went to play Bethany. It had snowed a little the afternoon of the game, but the snowing had stopped by the time we boarded the bus about five o'clock. We were all bundled up in our heaviest coats as we boarded, because we knew that it would take a long time for the heater to warm the spacious innards of the bus. There wasn't an open window to be seen. Everyone was intent on locking out as much of the cold as possible.

The guys on the bus usually fell into one of three categories on such trips. First there were the sleepers. Matt Tachsman and Andy Barjon could be relied upon to be dozing within a half hour of leaving Jewelton. Their ability to snooze despite the discomfort of the seats, the cold, the noise, and the less-than-effective shock absorbers was a continuing source of wonderment to the rest of us. Another group was made up of the games players. The Alpheson brothers and Tradeau were the long-standing members of that body. They always had some way of passing the time that involved contests or feats of skill. On the night of our bus ride to Bethany they were in the back trying to lob wadded-up pieces of paper into the knit cap that Pete had been wearing. This simulation of basketball shooting, they insisted, was necessary to stay "sharp" for that night's game. Pete wasn't willing at first to surrender his cap, but he relented when they insisted that he should do it for the good of the team. The rest of us fell into the category of talkers. Sometimes in twos, but more often in larger numbers, we carried on about school, girls, teachers, what we thought were new jokes, and any other subject that consciousness could imagine. It wasn't until we were within about 10 miles of our destination that Coach Levitson would predictably and loudly proclaim that it was time for us all to start thinking about the game and to squelch all chatter that was irrelevant to it.

The drive to Bethany took about an hour and 10 minutes at Coach Levitson's pace. As we tended to congregate at the back of the bus, our only contact with the Coach was to hear his continual, off-key whistling. He rarely whistled anything that we could identify, and when our conversation lagged, it was a standing joke to try to "Name That Tune." We had lots of laughs and arguments over what we thought he was trying to whistle. We learned early on that Coach himself could not settle any of the disputes about the titles of his melodies. We had sent people to the front of the bus a couple of times to ask him what the name was, and he never had any idea. "I'm just passing the time, Son, not conducting a concert" was the reply he once gave to me.

We had probably been on the road about 45 minutes when I felt the bus swerve sharply and heard the squeal of our brakes. The only memory I have of any other sound is that of the Coach's voice. His word was "No!" It was screamed as if it were a command to the bus to stop what it was about to do. But the bus did not stop. We could tell that it was leaning grotesquely to the right and was about to turn over. Then it flipped.

What I know about what follows comes from details of the State Police report, part of which was published in the paper, what others who were there told me, and what I experienced myself. The State Police said that a part of the steering mechanism broke as the bus rounded a curve. They noted that the bus was not traveling at an excessive speed when it went out of control, a fact that anyone who knew of Coach Levitson's driving habits could have told them in advance of the investigation. When the steering device broke, the bus apparently leaned too heavily on the right front tire and caused it to blow out. I saw that tire later when the bus was towed back to Jewelton, and it looked as if it had disintegrated. With the steering no longer responding and the tire in shreds, the bus hurtled off the road, despite Coach's stomping on the brake pedal and his screamed demand that it not get out of his control.

When the bus began to flip, all of us who were awake knew that we were in great danger. The sickening feeling of the top of the bus starting to exchange places with the bottom was immediately apparent. I remember the rolling over of the bus as one would recall any moment when life is threatened. Johnny was thrown into me. We slammed into a window and bounced off the ceiling. The moment of impact was upon us—the second when the bus would slam into the ditch, or the tree, or whatever was beside the road. But that moment did not come. I heard a ripping sound of metal against metal, and did not know what it meant.

The report from the State Police identified the bridge as number 42, a 70-foot-long construction over the Abana River. The report further noted that the bridge was ordinarily 15 feet above the usual level of the river. The information in the report states that because of recent rain and snowfall farther to the north, the river was about five feet above normal.

What the sound of metal against metal indicated, then, was that the bus had broken through the guard rail of the bridge just as it was leaning so precariously, and then fell into the Abana River. That explained why the sound of a crash did not come. The bus turned a complete revolution going off the bridge. It landed as if a hand had plucked it off the road, rotated it, and dropped it, tires first, into the water.

More than 50 years after the event, I still can feel the panic caused by the fall and the realization that we were in water. The bus's impact on the water sounded like an explosion, and I thought then that the motor had blown up—which it had not. The screaming still lingers in my ears, my own and that of all the others. The only words I remember as we hit the water were those of an unidentified voice yelling "Mama! Mama!" in its terror. The blackness was not immediate. I'm sure that the bus floated momentarily before it sank. Others recall this too, so I don't think we imagined it. Then the bus went down. The water at my feet was icy, and it prompted an absurd thought about my new shoes getting wet.

As we sank, the tiniest bit of rationality that anyone had left was destroyed. Since all the windows were closed, madness set in to open them and get out. If you know the construction of a school bus, you know how futile that attempt was. A school bus has windows that only open from the top—and only a few inches at that. This is obviously intended to prevent the window from being opened so wide that a child could fall out. No one was going to get out those windows!

The Abana River is typically 10 feet deep just below that bridge, but, rain-swollen, it was 15 feet deep that night. The bus settled to the bottom. There was air in the bus, but the water was getting in somewhere, and fast. Someone was wailing and trying to open a window, and someone else said we couldn't get out that way. The door at the front and the door at the rear were our escape routes. As we turned to the closer door at the rear, someone shouted that it was blocked. The police account of the wreck said that the last two seats, which had been jarred lose by the impact, had sealed up that exit. We were in water up to the chest. There was no light but we knew where the front of the bus was, and there was a mad drive to get there. No one was distinguishable. It was as if we had all become strangers. Brother could not help brother, friend did not know friend. To get out the front was imperative, and we actually had to swim to get there. We had become buoyant in the literal sense, floating and no longer in touch with the floor of the bus.

Someone screamed, "It's jammed!" He meant the front door. I could hear thrashing in the water and guessed that someone was fighting to free the door. The water was so cold by that time that I was becoming numb. I began to think my body would not be able to get me out the door even if it should be opened. I heard several people crying, and the fear was communicated from each of us to the other as we hung helpless between a door and our safety.

Then I could hear the Coach. He was sobbing, "God! Oh, God!" and I knew he was the one who was struggling in the darkness against the door. The police found that the handle, which is used to swing school-bus doors open and closed with very little effort by the driver, had been bent by the fall into the river. It was so distorted, its normal inward motion could not be brought about by yanking on it from the inside. But then I heard his shouted words, "It's open! Come on!"

When the door opened, the bus filled up with water. To survive required that each of us swim underwater with no light to guide us, find the door, and then make it 15 feet to the surface. Somehow it began to happen. I felt a hand pull me in the direction of the front and I reached for whoever was behind me and gave him a tug. I banged into what I knew was the windshield and was grateful for the pain, for I knew that the door was just to the right. I felt its outline, pulled myself through it, and headed for air. I have no tale to tell about lungs almost bursting—no words about how I feared I would die just before I could get to the top. What happened to me was not dramatic at all. I could only think of how easy it was to ascend, as soon as I got through that door. Once at the surface, I paddled toward the bank as I saw others doing, and I heard some of the other guys coming to the top behind me. I began to hyperventilate as I pulled myself out of the water. My breath was coming and going so rapidly that it seemed as if I couldn't breathe at all. The fear and the cold jumped on me with both feet, and I thought I would pass out. But then I heard Coach calling, loudly but calmly, for us all to come to him. He was on his knees, still partly in the water. I figured that he had been the last to get out. Whether he was the last or not was exactly what he was trying to determine. His voice shook with his body as he asked us, "Did everybody get out? How many are here?" In the dark we had no ready way to tell if all made it. He looked as if he were trying to count us, when Pete screamed in anguish, "Andy's not here!"

Coach commanded, "Wait! I've got to see if there's anybody else." His counting was so slow! The thought of Andy, somewhere in the bus, sickened me. Coach said with sadness that I'll never forget. "No. We're two short." The possibility of my going back into that water to try to find Andy and one other was something I couldn't face. I may have been the only one to think that way, and we never discussed it afterward, but I've wondered if any of us would have had the courage to go back. But we never had to find out whether we were that brave. Two heads appeared in the river.

Coach plowed through the water toward the pair and hauled in the one who was being supported by the other. Coach pulled the limp body of Andy to the bank and began to administer artificial respiration. Jesse walked out of the water unassisted. As we trembled in the freezing night, we watched Coach Levitson try, through artificial respiration, to give life to Andy. Carrying out the procedure exactly as I learned it in the Boy Scout Handbook, Coach put Andy on his stomach, turned his head to the side, and pressed hard on his back, trying to force water out and air in. He paused long enough to say, "Matt, you and Johnny go up to the highway and stop some cars. We've got to get out of this cold." The sight of him bending over Andy's body left me with the most powerless feeling I've ever experienced. There was nothing I could do to help. Then I thought to pray. At that moment, as Coach pushed hard on Andy's back and then lifted his arms, Andy made an indistinct sound, and then another, like a cough. Coach pounded his back. Andy coughed loudly and then he moaned. He was alive!

The aftermath of the wreck was an amalgam of people running down from the highway to help us, lots of orders being shouted, and finally being helped into cars and being taken to Bethany. Some of the cars that stopped were driven and occupied by horrified parents who were on the way to see their sons play. I heard it repeated over and over to the fearful parents: "Everybody's OK. Everybody's OK."

All of us were taken to the county hospital in Bethany and kept overnight for observation. Andy stayed another day as a precaution, but he was released in good condition. His survival under the waters of the Abana for a longer period than anyone else had to bear was attributed to, of all things, the coldness of the water. Pete told me later that a doctor told his mother and father that people often do not drown in or suffer brain damage in colder waters because their bodies react in some self-protective way to the cold. It sounded like an odd theory to me, but I was ready to accept anything given the fact that Andy was alive.

Newspapers all over the state reported the events of that night, and naturally they emphasized the part Jesse had played in saving Andy. He was a reluctant hero but could not avoid being interviewed and photographed.

Andy had no recollection of the wreck at all. He had been asleep when the wreck took place, and he couldn't recall anything that happened before he was put in a car for Bethany. Several reporters tried to get Jesse to explain how he had found Andy, how he had managed to get the larger boy out of the bus, how he had stayed under the water so long himself. Jesse pleaded that he could not account for any of it. He satisfied very few reporters with his answers, but they didn't persist. They wrote things like this, which was in our weekly paper: "The unassuming hero did not discuss his life-saving efforts in much detail. All that is known for sure is that without him, the accident would have been a tragedy."

It was many months later, after I had graduated, that I happened to be talking with Coach Levitson, and he told me that he withheld something from the State Police when they interviewed him about the matter.

"Luke, I tell you this because I think you'll believe it. I didn't tell the police because I thought that it was something that I should keep to myself. They asked me to tell them how I finally got the front door open. I told them I wasn't sure how it came open. They knew the handle had been bent, and they couldn't figure out how it ever popped loose. What I didn't say was that it was opened from the outside."

This was a revelation, but one that I couldn't fathom. I looked into the eyes of the man whose word was the most reliable I knew and asked, "But Coach, how could that have happened?"

"All I know is that I was getting nowhere with that door. It wasn't budging an inch. And then I felt the handle begin to move. I wasn't even pulling on it. Then the door opened. And I saw someone swim away from it. Now I know it was pitch dark down there, but I saw him anyway. It almost looked like a child—not much over five feet tall."

I couldn't believe what I was hearing! "Coach, are you telling me that Jesse opened the door? From the outside?"

He looked as positive as a man can look. "That is exactly what I'm telling you, Son. When Jesse didn't even want to discuss what we all knew he had done, namely, saving Andy's life, and when he said nothing about this other thing, then I figured I'd keep quiet too."

"But did you ever ask him about it?"

"No, I never really asked him directly about it. But I did bring it up once. A week or so later, one day after practice, I said, 'Jesse, we're all indebted to you for our lives.' He smiled and said, "You're welcome.""

I was bound up in the logical problems of what he was telling. How could a guy who weighed 105 pounds open a door that the Coach couldn't? The biggest difficulty, though, was the one I asked Coach to explain.

"How did he get outside? How could he have done that?"

Coach Levitson smiled, and I was aware that he had an answer, although I doubted if I could believe it. "Did you ever notice a cut on Jesse's back after the accident?" Remembering that I saw it when Jesse took off his jersey a few days after the wreck, I nodded that I had. "There's only one explanation, Son, as to how he got out. He went out a window."

I don't know if I believed it then, but I believe it now.

CHAPTER THIRTEEN

Jesse had become a celebrity in Jewelton. In a matter of weeks he had evolved from someone "known only to God and Mercer" to the best-known student in the school. His play against Cemaria in front of the home town fans had already sealed his name on many lips, and his rescue of Andy assured the fact that he was known to all.

People began inquiring into the phenomenon of Jesse Crosse. Where did he come from? Who were his parents? What kind of student was he? The transformation from the privacy of relative obscurity to the focus of public scrutiny was not an easy one for Jesse. That was typified by the newspaper interview set up for him by Mr. Abrams, our principal. Coach Levitson, who was also a subject of the interview, told me later that Jesse was obviously uncomfortable throughout the session, relaxing only when he could talk about other people. The local newspaper had begged Mr. Abrams to set up the question-and-answer period, because Jesse and his mother had previously turned down its requests. The paper wanted a follow-up on the story about the wreck, and Mr. Abrams was convinced that the publicity for the school was too good to pass up. He must have convinced Jesse of the same thing, for the interview was finally held.

I had to admit that I was like a lot of other people: thirsty for more information about Jewelton's boy in the spotlight. The newspaper story revealed that Jesse's mother, Maria Crosse, was a widow who supported the two of them by working as a nurse. Her husband, Joe, who had been a construction worker, died about two years before she and her son had moved to Jewelton. In the course of the interview, Coach Levitson informed the reporter that Jesse was an "excellent" student. Coach was quoted as saying that he mentioned that fact because he was sure Jesse wouldn't, and also because it refuted the popular belief that athletes did poorly in school. When I finished the article, I could tell that the reporter had been required to speculate to get a characterization of Jesse, so reluctant had his subject been in supplying details about himself.

The writer was forced to say, "The young man appears..." and "He seems..." and similar phrases which one must use when making guesses rather than supplying undisputed facts. I liked the article because it was written by a man who recognized that Jesse's humility was real, and that his primary interest in life was not self-promotion. It was a picture of Jesse to which I could say "Amen."

The game with Bethany had been cancelled, of course, and that meant that we were about to begin play with the nine teams in our league. Due to the small enrollments of the schools, the league was classified as Division B. There were three other classifications above us for the larger schools, with Triple A being the largest. In our state there were 40 teams in Division B, and four leagues in that division with 10 teams in each. We were in the B-West conference, which was considered one of the weaker ones, with the exception of teams from Charter House and Apollo, both of which had a history of respectable results in the state Class B tournaments. Whether it was a matter of alphabetical order or fate, the Anglers were to play Apollo first. Our primary test was a home game against the league's best.

The bus crash had taken place on Tuesday, and we had been counting on a week to prepare for the game with Apollo. Coach Levitson thought that the players were in no condition to practice until Friday, so that session and Monday's were the only ones we had to get ready for a perennial league champion. I had given up my custom of hanging out in the locker room to do homework—this was the first Anglers team I wanted to see as it prepared for the next opponent. Friday's practice was like a throw-back to the early days of the season. Coach Levitson ran them and ran them. I guess he decided that because they hadn't run since Monday they might be in danger of losing some of the conditioning they had built up.

The players were none too happy with that regimen; they had probably made the mistake of thinking that their first practice after the accident would be an easy one. It was anything but easy! Time after time they sprinted the floor. Then they had a short rest from the running to practice some plays. After that coach ordered them to run 25 laps around the gym. They paused to shoot some free throws. Then it was back to running. The sweat covered their jerseys first, and then their shorts. It wetted their hair and ran into their eyes. Coach was adamant and demanding: "You're too slow! Apollo is going to run you off the court! Faster!"

The players, even the four who I thought were capable of running all day, began to wilt badly. Their legs turned to wood. Their breathing was labored. I began to worry about someone getting sick again. Was this any way to treat people who had just been through a terrible experience? Finally, Coach Levitson relented and called for the final free throws. For the second time in a week they had been required to survive an ordeal. For the second time, they had.

Monday's practice was short and fun. Coach Levitson divided the team in half, with the two sides being approximately equal in talent and numbers (six versus seven). He had the two groups compete with each other at several tests of skill: layups, free throws, and jump shots from various spots on the court. The bunch that lost an event had to run two laps, accompanied by derisive comments and loud complaints from the winners that they were so slow Apollo was going to run them out of the gym. The surprise injection of these contests cheered up the sulky players, who had been making dire predictions before practice that Coach was probably going to "kill" them again as he had on Friday. When it was over, they left the locker room in high spirits, but I had to wonder why, at the last practice before our first conference game, Coach had run no plays and hadn't even mentioned the opponent. I decided that the older he got, the harder he was to figure out.

Apollo was the biggest of our league of small schools, with almost 100 more students than Jewelton had. It seemed to spend a great deal more money on sports than any other school in the conference. It may not have been so, but its players seemed to have new uniforms every year. I envied Apollo's organization, too. It had three managers and an assistant coach. When we played at its gym, its managers hauled out a metal rack on wheels that was full of what looked like brand new basketballs, putting our duffle bag and its worn contents to shame. Apollo's managers had enough shiny basketballs for each player to have his own when the team warmed up. Jewelton had but one good ball to match the twelve that Apollo had, and we saved that one for exclusive use in our home games. Our players got to handle it only when the other team was also eligible to use it.

Worst of all, the Suns were obviously able to match the quality of their basketballs with their players. They were mostly tall and sturdy-looking boys, with the exception of one burly, short one named Jeff Morris, a guard I recognized right away as the terror of the league the previous year. Built like a linebacker, Morris was amazingly quick and resourceful. He was an expert shooter from long range, and I knew that Si Montler and Jesse would have their hands full trying to cope with him.

Morris was someone to be feared, but I was agog at the sight of a Sun I had never seen before. He must have been 6-7. I spotted him as soon as the Suns came on the floor. He looked very young. I learned from the scorebook that his name was Hansen, and from the Suns' scorekeeper that he was only a sophomore. I watched him closely for signs that he was an undeveloped talent. I hoped to see him miss layups and bobble passes and run awkwardly. Not a sign. He looked like an accomplished senior in everything he did. When he came out on the floor to start the game, I knew that this was no budding player that Apollo hoped to develop for the future. The kid had already arrived.

As the Jewelton gym filled up early with fans eager to see the survivors and the hero of the wreck, our White unit took the floor first, as it had the past two games. Tom was dwarfed by Hansen at the center jump circle, and when Hansen showed on the tip-off that he was a fine leaper, I groaned at the prospect of having to deal with him for the full 32 minutes. The Suns worked the ball while our fans created a mighty din to distract them and encourage our boys. The players from Apollo were indifferent to the clamor. They functioned as if they didn't even see our players, much less hear our fans. After a few seconds, Hansen got the ball in front of the basket and made a ridiculously easy shot. Tom had been there to contend with him, but Hansen faked him totally out of position and dropped it in. I looked down the bench, from my spot at the end, past seven grim players' faces to see the grimmest face of all: Coach Levitson's. We had really run into a buzz-saw!

Si brought the ball up against Morris, who was virtually snorting like a bull with aggressiveness. Si looked unsure of himself as Morris shadowed his every move. Morris was immediately on him as Si stopped his dribble to pass. Morris jolted the ball from his hands, whirled around him, batted the ball toward the Suns' goal, and was off to an uncontested layup. It was 4-0 and looked as if it wasn't going to get much better very fast, as once again Si had the unenviable job of getting past Morris. If anything, Morris's first steal seemed to stimulate him to even more tenacious defense. As he passed me on the bench while he was challenging Si's dribble up court, Morris was emitting sounds that reminded me of growling. He was a very rough customer! While Si was dribbling, Morris swatted the ball off Si's leg and it was headed out of bounds. Determined not to turn the ball over to Apollo again, Si made a dash for it and was able to flip it back in bounds to Phil Lipscomb. Si's leap took place at the conjunction of the center line and the sideline, and he slammed into the scorer's table. Normally such acrobatics are followed by the player being righted by the people he has crashed into, and he returns quickly to the court.

But Si didn't get up. He was hurt. The referee saw that Si was injured and
called time out. Si's hip was already a painful-looking red as we treated him
where he lay. He was trying to tough it out, but he flinched as Coach touched
the point of impact, and Si admitted that his left leg felt numb. He wasn't
likely to play again that night. Pete and Coach Levitson picked him up and
took him to the dressing room, with Coach saying over his shoulder as he left,
"Crosse: in for Montler."

So we were down to one point guard who would try to deal with Morris
for the rest of the game. I had been consoling myself before Si's injury that at
least we could keep a fresh player in the game against Morris. I had an idea
that the two of them could wear Morris down some as the game went on. Now
that strategy was shot. Thirty of the game's minutes remained, and Jesse had
Morris all to himself.

Lipscomb took the ball from the referee and looked to in-bound it.
Morris was chasing Jesse, who was trying to free himself to receive the pass.
Phil decided that he didn't want to tempt fate by throwing the ball anywhere
near Morris, so he fired it to Tom, who had broken clear of Hansen. Tom
turned to our goal, holding the ball over his head with two hands. I couldn't
think of what he was doing when he let it fly toward our basket—there was no
one there to catch it! Then I saw that Jesse, who had probably seemed rather
unimportant to Morris, had gotten free from him and all the rest of the Suns,
too. He streaked for the pass, got it at full speed, and nonchalantly scored
his first basket of the year! Our fans bellowed their happiness at the turn of
events. The reed-like sophomore had out-foxed the veteran.

Morris had an "it won't happen again" look as he initiated the Suns'
offensive patterns. The rest of Apollo's team acted as if nothing had happened.
They were in the process of inching closer and closer to the goal, with a pass to
the skyscraping Hansen becoming more and more likely, when Jesse stripped
the ball away from Morris. Morris had seemed disdainful of Jesse and had
been trying hard to ignore him. He was too casual, however, and Jesse made
him pay for it. Jesse raced to the Jewelton goal, with Morris in hot pursuit.
Jesse was in his highest gear, but I had to admit that Morris was matching
him step for step. As they hurtled to the goal, I was sure that Morris would
either foul Jesse as he attempted a layup or block his shot. A third possibility
had not entered my mind. Just as the two got to the spot where the shot would
normally have originated, Jesse hit the brakes, full force. Caught completely
unaware, Morris's body obeyed the very laws of physics which Jesse's had
seemingly just violated. Morris catapulted ahead, did a headfirst tumble, and
slid to a spot beyond the goal on his hands and knees. Not even bothering to

jump, Jesse calmly shot the ball softly off the backboard and through.

Since the word "bedlam" comes from the name of an English hospital for the insane, that makes it the best word I could possibly use to describe the outburst which followed that basket. The Jewelton fans, who were probably 80% of those present, sent up such a roar that it sounded like a fleet of jets blasting inside an airplane hangar.

The first quarter ended with the Suns ahead by only two points. Morris was evidencing a new respect for Jesse, and he was no longer doing his animal imitation on defense, as far as I could hear. When the Red group replaced the White at the start of the second quarter, Jesse stayed in the game. Coach told us that Si wouldn't be back for sure; his leg was still numb. Jesse was drenched with sweat but looked as calm as if he were at practice.

The real thorn in our side during the first period had been Hansen. After looking pretty bad on the two plays involving Jesse, Morris had gone low profile and contented himself with making passes to his tall teammate near the goal. It would be Pete's challenge to take on Hansen in the second period.

Although Pete was about five inches shorter than Hansen, I knew he was determined to slow him down. Pete was at his best when facing a challenge. The Apollo team, not being familiar with Coach Levitson's substation plans, may have thought we were starting the second quarter with some players of lesser talent, to give four starters a rest. At any rate, the Suns looked very relaxed again as the period started. They had shown some anxiety as the Anglers stayed close throughout the first eight minutes, but they began the second stanza as they had the first, with Hansen easily tipping the ball to Morris. When Pete put a resounding block on Hansen's first field-goal try, our fans exploded again. The blocked shot bounced all the way to the center line where Jesse gobbled it up and fed Johnny for the tying shot.

The Suns settled down to serious business right then and there. They weren't taking anything for granted anymore. They were excellent players; they would do what was necessary to win. The second quarter was a memorable struggle. Their big guns, Morris and Hansen, played with renewed determination and much success. Pete blocked no more shots, as Hansen was much more careful when he made his attempts. Our guys worked several fast breaks with dazzling effect, with Jesse leading almost every charge. We also manufactured a few baskets with the patient offense that undoubtedly caught the Suns off guard. We tied them just at the buzzer, with the Anglers working the final 60 seconds off the clock to try for the last shot. Bart Holeman took a pass from Jimmy Alpheson with only seconds to go, and he ignited the dynamite in the stands once more with a nifty jump shot from 10 feet. The game was, as my father often said about the weather, "as hot as a two-dollar pistol." The score was even at 30.

CHAPTER FOURTEEN

I was disturbed by the scene in the locker room at halftime. The shot that tied the score appeared to affect the players and Coach the same way: They acted as if we had won the game rather than having just caught up. I thought the optimism was premature and too unrestrained. The faces of Apollo's players as they went to their dressing room were fresh in my mind. If ever I saw a resolute team, the Suns fit that description. We had played them close on a couple of occasions during my time with the Anglers, and they had invariably blasted us in the late stages of the game. They had history on their side; we had the excitement of the moment.

Coach Levitson was handing out praise and pats on the back. He was not urging caution, as I thought he should have been. The only sobering moment came when he told the team that Si had to be taken to the hospital to have his leg examined. He didn't dwell on that, however, and he quickly reverted to comments about how pleased he was with the first-half action. I thrust the statistics from the half upon him, hoping he would notice that Hansen already had 16 points. Something had to be done to stop him. Aside from Pete's block of one shot, we hadn't been able to thwart the towering center.

Coach glanced at the numbers briefly but made no remarks about them. He urged the players to continue to play as they had. He especially encouraged them to keep watching for a teammate who had the better, closer shot. "And keep on running whenever you get a chance. Remember, there isn't a player on the floor who can run as fast as a pass can fly through the air. Look down court for your teammate." He had taken off his gray sport coat and was energetically drawing plays and patterns on the blackboard. No significant mention of the Suns was made. It was as if they wouldn't even be on the court for the second half. Why was he ignoring them?

The few minutes of rest and constant wiping with towels had cooled off

the players, and that is exactly what I had qualms about in a different sense—
that we would cool off at the start of the third quarter, and Apollo would pull
away from us. Coach Levitson concluded the intermission by asking the team
to play as hard as Si had when he got hurt. "Boys, you experience the joy of
this game only when you know in your heart that you're giving all you've got
for the benefit of everybody else. When that happens, you've found the secret
of this or any team sport. Now, let's go out there and have some fun!" For
the second time in the young season, Coach was talking about "fun" when
I thought he should be discussing the tough job of beating the other team.

The players whooped and hollered and burst out of the locker room,
headed for what I feared was a big come-down. I remained to gather up the
towels. Coach was putting his coat back on. I guess I had a disapproving
look on my face. He spoke softly to me: "Son, I believe I know what you're
thinking. You think I should have told them to come back to earth and to
watch out that Apollo doesn't blow us off the court, don't you?" I nodded my
firm agreement to that.

"Luke, this team is probably not going to win this game. Apollo is just
too good. But if we lose, I want it to be with our boys playing all-out. I don't
want them playing scared. If I spent my time reminding them of how good
Apollo is, it would get them thinking about the other team instead of ours. I
don't want them to do that. These kids are on the threshold of becoming a real
team—13 boys pulling together, for each other. It doesn't happen very often. If
we develop that spirit, it doesn't matter how many games we win. We'll have
the satisfaction of knowing that we played the game right. That's something
they won't forget. Can you see what I'm shooting for?"

I could. And I was embarrassed and pleased at the same time. I was
ashamed to admit to myself that all that counted to me was this game, not the
long-range goals that Coach had in mind. But I felt honored that he thought I
merited an explanation. He talked to me as if I were more than just the keeper
of the towels and basketballs and statistics. He wanted me to understand, and
I did.

"Coach, why do you suppose it takes me so long to catch on? You really
ought to pick a smarter manager next year." He slapped me on the back and
laughed as we left, saying, "Son, you're absolutely right!"

I suspected from the grim looks on the Suns' faces that their coach
had really chewed them out in the dressing room. Even the youthful face of
Hansen had a scowl on it, and Morris seemed snorting mad again after going
relatively meek in the second quarter. Hansen skyrocketed for the opening tip
and slapped the ball so hard that he almost knocked it over Morris's head and

out of bounds. Morris managed to catch up with the ball, and he confidently dribbled it toward Jesse.

When he was on defense, Jesse crouched so low that he cut his already short stature in half. His head was about at the height of Morris's waist, and it was hard to account for his ability to move so fast from that position. His hands constantly flicked at the ball as it bounded from the hand of Morris to the floor. He swatted Morris's dribble out of bounds, temporarily slowing the Suns' attack. After Apollo threw the ball in, Jesse knocked it out again! Morris was tiring of the opposition that Jesse was providing, and on the third try he put his head down and charged for the goal. And charge he did, as Jesse sensed the move and planted his feet to cause the hard-driving Morris to commit an offensive foul when he bashed Jesse. After Morris was called for charging, the Anglers had their first opportunity to take the lead. Our crowd was imploring them to surpass the Suns, and they weren't disappointed.

Ten or 12 passes into the maddeningly patient offense, Jesse faked one way, then roared past the now baffled Morris and flew to the goal. Hansen, who by my quick estimate was almost a foot-and-a-half taller than Jesse, moved with startling quickness to cut off the black dart heading to the basket. No sooner had Hansen left his man to cover Jesse, than Jesse flipped a bounce pass to Tom for a wide-open layup. The fans roared as much for the pass as the shot, because Jesse had bounced the ball between Hansen's legs! I almost felt sorry for the highly-elevated Apollo center, for it was clear that he had no idea of where the ball had gone. He never saw it split his gangly legs, and he could only assume from the sustained cheering that Jewelton had scored.

The third quarter was a contrast to the first two. Apollo played very cautiously, and our conservative offense wasn't getting many shots either. The 42-40 score after three periods remained in our favor. I prayed that we could nurse it along for eight more minutes. The brief rest between quarters was the time for Coach Levitson to have his say about our strategy for the home stretch. The Red team members were energized by what the Whites had done, and they pledged to hold the lead. I had been offering towels to the proud, exhausted White crew and was late getting to Coach's huddle with the Reds.

Coach Levitson was on the verge of our league's biggest upset in years, if we could only hang on—could just keep doing what we'd been doing. So what was he up to in the huddle? He was telling the Reds that the time had come to go whole-hog for the fast break! While I was contemplating a stall offense to stay close to Apollo, he was telling them to run wild. He reminded them that, with the exception of Jesse, they were all well rested, and there should be no reason why they couldn't go full blast for eight minutes. My doubts were not shared by the players, however. They grinned approvingly at his instructions, nodding vigorously at his suggestion that they should be able to go all-out. Only Jesse wasn't indicating any enthusiasm. He had played every minute since Si was hurt. His head was bowed with fatigue, and his uniform hung limply from the sweat. His unrelenting effort had taken its toll. Coach Levitson saw his little guard's weariness and asked him if he wanted a rest.

"No thanks, Coach. I'm OK," was his reply. I had to wonder if Jesse was making a wise decision. He was in serious need of more than the break between quarters. The buzzer waits for no man, however, and it notified all that the crucial quarter was upon us.

The delirious Jewelton fans swept our five back onto the court with their raucous support. As if through a telescope, I could clearly see various people in the stands. Mr. Abrams, the principal, was vigorously pounding one hand with his rolled up program. My mother and father were talking animatedly with a woman I would later learn was Jesse's mother. Carol Smith, my current favorite female of them all, was standing with eight crossed fingers to evoke all the good luck she could. It was a picture of enthusiasm and aspiration that was new to Jewelton. Our five-man band was booming away with "Happy Days Are Here Again," but I knew that the next eight minutes would determine whether that was so.

Morris got the ball for Apollo and, for the first time that night, really got away from Jesse, to score the tying basket. Jesse was not his former self as we tried to regain the lead. I could tell that he was making a supreme effort, but he had lost his usual zing. He tried a long pass to Jimmy Alpheson and threw it behind him and out of bounds. Coach Levitson called timeout.

At the bench, Coach scrutinized Jesse closely. Usually the players stood with Coach during timeouts, but this time he told them to sit. Jesse wasn't recovering very fast, and when the buzzer signaled that play was to start, Coach Levitson called another timeout! I tried to tell him that he was about to use up our last one, but he either didn't hear or didn't care. He was taking a huge gamble. Jesse's recuperation was paramount in his mind, despite the fact that there were seven minutes left, and we wouldn't be able to stop the clock again. I have to admit that the second timeout did Jesse a lot of good. He perked up considerably, and we took the floor with the score tied, and the ball belonging to the Suns.

I was surprised when one of Apollo's lesser players took their next shot, and the Apollo coach was obviously disgusted by it. He flung a towel to the floor as the ball bounced off the rim. Bart Holeman rebounded and passed to Jesse. The break was on! Jesse was apparently back to normal as he streaked up the middle of the court. He zigzagged around Morris and could have taken the shot himself, but he underhanded it to Pete for the two points.

The next six minutes were a nightmare—for Apollo. The Anglers were at the top of their game, and the Suns couldn't stop them. The fast-break tactic did "bedazzle" them, just as coach had predicted weeks before that it would. The lead expanded to eight, and then 10 points. The Suns were too good a team to quit, but the life had gone out of them. On one play, Jesse picked Morris's pocket once again, and the Suns' guard turned to his coach on the bench and shrugged his shoulders as if saying that he didn't know how to cope with Jesse anymore. The coach offered him no advice. He just slumped back in his seat as Jim Wirges got the basket when Jesse spotted him for yet another hurry-up score.

With a minute to play and the Anglers leading 61-50, Coach inserted Tradeau for Jesse. The cheers for Jesse were unrelenting. The ovation extended beyond the resumption of play. Jesse sat with me at the end of the bench, and I could feel the applause and shouting as much as I could hear it. The game ended with our first win over Apollo in nine years. The margin was nine points, and we were wild with happiness until we got back to the dressing room. A window to the outside had been shattered, the glass littering the floor. Clothes had been thrown about, a trash can had been tipped over, and crudely painted on the wall in still-wet black letters was, "Watch out nigger! KKK"

CHAPTER FIFTEEN

The impact of those words on the wall was like a kick in the stomach. We were momentarily struck dumb and immobile by the message of hate. Coach Levitson hadn't yet returned to the locker room, so we were left to deal with it ourselves. Pete was the first to respond. He grabbed a towel from the stack I had placed on the bench near the shower room. He said nothing but his intent was evident. He attacked the black paint. The resulting smear was ugly to see, but not so ugly as what it replaced. Coach entered at that moment and was confounded by the silence and the sight of all of us watching Pete obliterate the obscenity.

"Boys, what's going on here?" he demanded. It wasn't something that anyone wanted to repeat. The quiet was broken by Johnny. "Coach, someone broke in here and wrote a threat on the wall against Jesse." Pete was still at the sink with the befouled towel, and he wheeled angrily and spoke for all of us: "Coach, this makes me sick. I think you ought to call the police. They shouldn't get away with it."

"I will call the police, Son. We'll find out who did it. I want you all to shower now, and then wait for me. I'll be back in just a few minutes. Luke, will you bring the basketballs to my office?" He left without requesting more information. I expected that he would get it from me.

In his office when I told him what had been on the wall, he put his head in his hands. When he looked up from his desk it was to locate the telephone directory. He found the police department number, dialed it, and reported a break-in and defacement of school property. He didn't give the details of the writing on the wall. He seemed satisfied by the response at the other end of the line and thanked whomever he was talking to. He asked me what was the reaction of the team, and the best description I could give was "shock."

"How did Jesse respond, Son? Did you happen to notice?"

I told him that I was too embarrassed to look. I assumed that Jesse was as stunned as the rest of us, but what else the graffiti had done to him, I couldn't say. My assumption was that someone who was white, someone whose skin was like mine, had manufactured the crudely lettered slur. To a certain extent then, I was ashamed for what someone like me had done. It was a shared guilt. I hadn't been able to face Jesse. I didn't reveal the guilty feeling to the coach, however, and I stood mutely before him, trusting that he knew the right thing to do under the circumstances. He was fiddling with papers on his desk and wasn't paying much attention to me. I didn't know whether to stay or to go, and his puttering wasn't giving me any clue. Then he looked up and said, "Will you let me know when everyone has had a shower and is dressed?"

When I got back to the locker room, everyone was seated and waiting for Coach. If they had showered, it was in record time. They seemed eager, like me, to have Coach help us to understand and cope with what had happened. For the first time I looked at Jesse. His face showed no emotion. He was sitting very still, in contrast to a lot of agitated motion by the rest. I went back to his office and told Coach we were ready.

With his sport coat off again, I was reminded of the halftime that seemed so long ago and so unimportant in the face of what had happened. He was as serious as I had ever seen him.

"Boys, we had a big challenge tonight when we played Apollo. And we were equal to that challenge. But, as you have seen, we have an even bigger challenge in front of us. What was probably the work of only one sick person has shown us that it takes a lot of good to overcome evil. Tonight you have come face-to-face, some of you for the first time, with one of the worst of all the traits of a human being: racism."

My sidelong glance at our team confirmed that Coach had undivided attention, except that Jesse's gaze was directed at the floor. My anger rose at how the incident had robbed him and the others of the joy of that night. Just then there was a knock on the locker room door. At first I thought it was the police, but when I went to answer it, I realized that there were large numbers of parents and well-wishers outside, waiting for the victors to emerge. They were still full of exuberance, as was evident from the fact that they cheered even me when I appeared at the door.

"What's keeping you guys, Luke? Tell the big winners we want to see them!" This and other comments like it I brushed aside, telling them we were having a team meeting and would be out soon. I quickly returned to my place, and Coach resumed.

"The first challenge we have to face is the fact that we'd probably like to sweep this under the carpet and hope to never see it again. We can't do that. We have to face this. Jesse?"

At the mention of his name, Jesse raised his head and looked directly at Coach. "Jesse, I want to apologize to you for what somebody did. But I think I'm to blame, too. If I don't fight this sort of thing, and I confess to you that I haven't always, then I participate in it, if only because it grows when people say little or nothing about it. I'm sorry."

Jesse nodded in Coach's direction as the apology was made. I realized that he wasn't treating Coach's words as just a speech. He was taking the apology at face value and responding with forgiveness. Coach had touched my own feelings of guilt. He was going deeper than I really cared to go. His apology was one which I felt the need to express, but I wasn't confident I had the courage to do it. Then Pete, able as usual to do the right thing, stood up and faced Jesse.

"I'm sorry, too, Jesse."

With that he sat, and the rest of us pondered what to do next. The thought of each of us professing our shame was awkward. Then Johnny, moved by Coach's words and Pete's response, got up from the other end of the bench from Jesse and walked to him and shook his hand. This symbolic act crystallized for the rest of us what we could do. We followed Johnny's example. There were no words exchanged—just hands clasped.

Coach Levitson said, "Boys, there is one other challenge we must face. The Ku Klux Klan may really be behind this." Those words chilled me. The Klan? I knew it had once existed in our area, but I assumed that it had long since died out.

"If this isn't just the work of one deranged person," Coach continued, "then we will have to stand against whatever is to come. We can see tonight that there are matters more important than basketball; we are a team, and all of us together can handle more than each of us can by himself. I hope the police will be able to find out what this is all about. Until we learn more, I suggest you recognize that even if it is only one person who is trying to get at Jesse, that he is attacking us all. It's no doubt because Jesse is part of this team that someone has chosen to threaten him. So we have all been threatened. No one is an island in this—we should face this as a team of 13."

"Fourteen." I interrupted, which caused the others to laugh, and Coach Levitson to bow to my insistence that I be included. Pete, who had seized the reins twice already, grabbed them once again.

"Coach, I know it's your custom to let the seniors alternate as captains for each game. You've done that ever since I was a sophomore, and probably for a long time before that."

Pete's implication that Coach Levitson had been around for eons provoked the rest of us to smile at his unintended suggestion. A moment of humor at that time was appreciated. Coach, going along with the diversion, held his heart as if he had been hurt by the suggestion that he was ancient, but Pete was undeterred.

"You know what I mean, Coach. Anyhow, I'd like to ask you to allow us to vote tonight for a permanent captain for the rest of the year. I want to nominate Jesse for two reasons. First of all, he's the one who convinced us that your offense would work. I know that nobody's ever said this out loud, but the main reason we're better this year is because Jesse showed us that a pass was as good as a shot. Before this season began, I thought that we'd win about five games, and all I could think of was trying to get as many points as I could. Now I don't care about that any more. I'd trade a win over Apollo for points any day. I mean, it was really great, wasn't it?"

At this declaration, the rest of us cheered loudly, bringing back for the moment the happiness that the victory over the Suns had created. Pete had another comment to add. "The second reason I think we should elect him is to show whoever it was who got in here tonight that we are backing Jesse 100%. We can show that jerk that all he did was bring us even closer together than we were before. Would that be OK, Coach?"

Coach Levitson looked surprised by the suggestion, but as others were on their feet seconding Pete, he recognized an idea whose time had come, and said, "If that's the feeling of the team, then I'm in agreement. Now, get out of here and try to enjoy all that you've done tonight, both during the game and after. For the time being, don't talk to anyone not on the team about what happened here until we've had time for the police to look into it. Is that clear? Talk to no one. See you at practice tomorrow."

The meeting ended with a cheer, and the players exited to the yells of the crowd that had remained outside the dressing room through it all. I could hear the inquiries, "What's been going on in there?" and replies like, "Just a private team meeting." I wondered if the silence that Coach had requested would hold.

He asked me to stay until the police had come, to give an eyewitness report to the writing on the wall. He went outside into the gym to look for the police, and I began to sweep up the broken glass, trying to think of what was the best way to dispose of the paint-soaked towel. I was just about to throw it in the trash bin that I had uprighted, when I heard a voice behind me state sharply, "Don't throw that away! It might be evidence."

I was startled as I whirled to see a young policeman peering over Coach's shoulder as they entered. He didn't look very much older than 20, and as he approached I could read the name "Smith" on a plastic tag attached to his shirt. I didn't know Jewelton had policemen so young, nor did I know until then that we had any who were black.

Officer Smith surveyed the scene quickly and began to ask questions and take notes. He was a bit perturbed that I had cleared away the glass. He wanted to know in what way it had been scattered, apparently trying to determine how the window had been broken. He turned his attention to the smudged wall and asked what had been written there. I paused only a second, and then blurted out the inscription. He wrote it without missing a beat. He asked if I could find a paper bag in which he might place the towel. He wanted Coach to estimate when the entry had taken place, and then he said he was going outside to examine where the intruder or intruders had gotten in. He requested that we wait for his return.

He was gone longer than I thought he would be. Coach Levitson and I sat on the players' benches at the lockers and said very little, mostly comments that affirmed our disbelief that the break-in had occurred and our inability to understand what motivated such a thing.

When Smith returned, he asked us if we had any ideas about who might have done it. Of course we didn't. He looked to be at the end of his investigation, and I could tell that Coach Levitson wanted a turn to question him.

"Officer, what do you make of this Klan business? Is that just a smokescreen to throw us off the trail?"

Officer Smith responded in a non-committal way. "It's not possible to determine that at this time. There isn't enough evidence to reach a conclusion."

His official manner didn't satisfy Coach. He wanted more than just a dry recitation of the facts. He tried again: "I know you can't tell for sure, I just want your opinion of what happened here tonight. Have you heard anything to lead you to believe that the Klan is back in business in these parts? We've got a 15-year-old boy on this team that I'm worried about."

Coach Levitson's interest had almost become anger. He was impatient with Officer Smith's detached approach, and the policeman could tell that Coach was deeply concerned. Smith's manner changed altogether. I think he was waiting to be certain that Coach Levitson was committed to Jesse's welfare before he revealed his feelings. He looked at me and apparently decided that he could trust that my sentiments were the same as Coach's.

"Coach, people don't talk about the Klan around here. That doesn't mean it doesn't exist. I've investigated two other incidents like this. On both occasions there was a Klan calling card left behind. Nobody else on the force thinks the Klan is back. That's why neither of the other incidents was reported in the paper as having any Klan connection."

Coach Levitson was gravely taking in Smith's account.

He summarized what he thought he had been hearing: "Officer Smith, I think you're saying that you think the Klan is back, but that your feelings are not shared by the other policemen, even the chief. This is all off-the-record as far as the boy and I are concerned. Will you tell me how seriously you think we should take this threat?"

"Very seriously."

CHAPTER SIXTEEN

The story of the racial threat painted on the locker room wall was circulating widely and wildly by the following day. Coach's request for sealed lips obviously was not honored by one or more team members. The rumor mill was working overtime. One account had it that the players were met in the dressing room by three armed, hooded Klansmen, and that they left only after waving guns under our noses. All the players I happened to see during the day swore that they had not broken the silence. We were hard pressed to know how to cope with the rumors. If we told what happened in an effort to correct them, we would be going against Coach's desire that we not talk. But if we didn't set the record straight, we feared that the incident would be blown hopelessly out of proportion.

As sixth period classes began that Wednesday, there was an interruption of all classes by an intercom announcement from Mr. Abrams. He acknowledged that there had been a break-in of the locker room the night before, and that someone had painted on the wall. He stressed that no student had been threatened with a gun, and that students should refrain from fanciful gossip about the situation. He noted that the police were investigating, and that he hoped the matter would be shortly cleared up. He encouraged the students to talk about the night before all they wanted—as long as they confined themselves to the upset of Apollo.

The mention of the victory brought shouts of approval from all the classrooms and put the focus back on the game, and not its aftermath. I was relieved that Mr. Abrams' discussion of the affair had clarified events and had blunted the students' inquiry into them. I knew it was probably useless to conjecture about who had leaked the story, but I was mad at him or them for betraying the confidentiality Coach had requested. Despite the talk about how the team had come together, someone found it more important to spread a spicy story than keep his lip buttoned for the good of the team. That bothered me—mostly because it created suspicion in my mind against several players who I thought capable of such a thing, but most of whom I knew had probably not broken their word. I didn't like being suspicious, but I couldn't help it.

If I was disturbed by the fact that someone blabbed, Coach Levitson was furious. He was waiting for us in the locker room when we got there after school. Remembering the last time he had been there, I was positive that once more he was going to tear into us. He curtly told us not to get ready for practice. "Just sit" was his command.

As later arriving players jauntily entered the dressing room, they were abruptly separated from their high spirits by the sight of the rest of us benched, and obviously waiting for the bawling out that was to come. They took their places without a word, and when all were there, we braced ourselves.

He was smoldering, but he was under control. Coach's words were restrained and all the more effective because he was so evidently fighting to not let his feelings get the better of him.

"Someone in this room has done a disservice to us all. His talk about last night's episode makes it very unlikely that we will catch the perpetrator if that person was a student at this school. If no one had talked, whoever broke in here last night would probably have talked about it. Calling until midnight last night, Mr. Abrams and I contacted several reliable students, asking them to be listening for any unusual stories about something that happened after the game. None of those students knew what we were looking for; they just agreed to keep their ears open. Now that network of kids, who would have been glad to help us find the person or persons who did this, is useless. They won't hear anybody bragging about what he did because it was necessary for Mr. Abrams to make his announcement just to keep the rumors from going totally out of control. Whoever broke in last night is probably not going to reveal himself now that his deed has been publicized. Our only hope was that our silence about it would have flushed him out."

I was surprised to discover how little I had understood about how the squealer had messed things up. Whatever his reason might have been for talking, however innocent it might have been, he had made a huge mistake.

Coach concluded his remarks by saying, "I don't know how many of you talked, but you have put yourself before the team. I'm not going to conduct a witch hunt to try to find out who you are, but I think it would do you a lot of good if you came to me and told me that you did it. I will not reveal your name to the other boys, but it would set our minds to rest if you were to identify yourself. It would show everyone that you are willing to own up to your mistake. It would go a long way to restoring trust on this team if you did that. I will tell the rest of the team that you have spoken to me, but I will never tell them who you are."

Coach Levitson was never to announce that a confession had been made. We may have put that in the back of our minds, but as the days turned to weeks without any notification from him that someone had stepped forward, we were always aware that whoever had done it was unwilling to set matters straight. The weed of doubt was never exterminated.

By Thursday, there wasn't much talk at school about the break-in. I was setting my sights on our next game, a trip to Cane Creek on Friday night. I presumed that if people were talking about basketball, it was concerning the prospect of winning our second league game. At lunch on Thursday, Carol, my girlfriend, pointed out to me that the hottest topic of conversation was only indirectly related to basketball.

"Luke, are you aware of all the talk that's going around about Jesse?" Carol wasn't one to approach a touchy subject straightforwardly. She sneaked up on it from the side. I assumed that she meant that he had been threatened, and assured her that I was up-to-date on it all. She immediately let me know that story was old news. I had no idea what she was getting at, but I decided it couldn't be too important since I hadn't heard it. Carol looked genuinely distressed that I didn't show more concern.

"Luke, I don't think you realize how serious this is!" The alarm in her voice alerted me to her worry.

"What are you talking about?" I asked. She edged closer to me at the table where we were eating and pointed for only a split second to a corner of the room customarily occupied by sophomores. I looked in the direction known as the "Sophomore Swamp" and saw Jesse at a table. I grasped no significance from what I could see.

"What are you pointing at, Carol? Is the big gossip that Jesse eats lunch? I know he's done some amazing things lately, but he has to eat just like the rest of us mortals."

Carol wasn't happy with my flip comment, and she let me know it. "Damn it, Luke, Jesse is with *her*!" It wasn't like Carol to cuss, and I quickly glanced back to Jesse's table. There was a girl with her back to me whom I suddenly recognized. As I write this many years after the fact, I am inclined to shy away from some of the details because they may cause pain to someone who reads this. But I have to tell the basics of what follows because they are vital to the story. The girl who was sitting across the table from Jesse, at a table where no others sat, is someone I will identify as "Maggie." I don't know what has become of Maggie, but she disappeared from Jewelton soon after she graduated. Her role in this cannot be omitted, however much I wish I did not have to bring it up.

Maggie was the subject of a great deal of talk. She was a senior, and for the past two years her reputation was that of a girl infatuated with basketball players. She may have suffered very unfairly at the mercy of people who never bothered to find out the truth about her. She was reportedly a pushover for Angler players, and I had heard her name bandied about by team members ever since she was a sophomore. The boasting that went on about her was incessant, with boys trying to out-do each other with their tales about Maggie.

As a 10th grader I was inclined to believe all that I heard about her, but as I got older I began to believe that much of the talk was merely hot air. But the damage had been done. Like a lot of other thoughtless people, I had believed the naïve notion that where there was smoke there must be at least a little fire. It was true that Maggie had dated some of the players from time to time, but teen-aged boys can be very imaginative when it comes to telling stories about their romantic exploits. By the time I was a senior, I guess I would describe my attitude toward Maggie as one of mixed emotions. On the one hand, I found her a very lively and likable girl on the few occasions I had to talk to her. But on the other, I was still inclined to categorize her as one of those girls "you wouldn't want to take home to Mom and Dad." I was guilty of believing enough of the rumors that I had separated her in my mind from the "nice" girls in our class.

I was looking at Maggie and Jesse, and I knew what the gossip must be. "How long has that been going on?" I asked Carol. She shrugged her shoulders to indicate that she wasn't certain. She did say that she had seen the two of them sitting together at a table by themselves the day before. I wasn't jumping to any conclusions, but I felt a kind of dread because the situation didn't have any saving graces that I could see.

To my knowledge, by the year 1960, no black and white students at Jewelton had ever dated each other. Not only had students of opposite sexes and races not ever been out together, but students of the same gender but different colors were rarely seen in each other's company in public. The story that Tradeau told of Jesse and his three white friends eating at Jesse's house was a highly unusual social arrangement at that time. The races seemed to have an understanding that they would not mix. There was no open hostility, but there was not much that could be classified as friendliness either. I knew that the sight of Jesse and Maggie would have stirred up the kinds of people who are at one and the same time offended and stimulated by such things. If ever there was an item that would evoke excited talk, this was it.

Carol looked at me expectantly, as if she was waiting for my analysis of how to deal with the matter. "What do you want me to do about it?" I demanded. I think we were both a little surprised at how crossly I said those words. I didn't know how to resolve the problems of race and reputation, but I knew that unless someone did, there was going to be trouble. My irritation was that I could see it coming, but didn't know how to stop it.

Carol flinched at my frustrated response and mumbled that I was getting grouchy, and that she thought I would have appreciated her pointing out the situation. She swiftly departed from the table and me. I was left with my peanut butter and jelly and the strong wish that Carol hadn't said anything at all.

At practice that afternoon Coach told the players a bit about what to expect from Cane Creek and urged the team not to take it lightly, just because Apollo had lost to us. Cane Creek was usually a lower echelon team like Jewelton, but Coach warned that if we could beat Apollo, then anything could happen. Despite his admonitions, I could tell that the players weren't taking Coach's words to heart. They were very relaxed, and if I had ever before experienced a Jewelton team which was overconfident, which I hadn't, I think I would have said that we were at that stage on the eve of the game with the Cougars.

Despite the outburst at Carol, and denying any way of dealing with the Jesse and Maggie situation, I hoped to catch Coach Levitson after practice to talk to him about it. He was still in his office after all the players had gone, and I asked him if we could talk. When I closed the door as I went in, he registered a look of surprise. He told me to sit, and I realized he may have been wondering if I were about to concede that I had been the one to spill the beans about the break-in. I wanted to discourage that possibility right away.

"Coach, this doesn't have anything to do with the other night. It's about something new that I think you ought to know about." He eased back in his battered chair and said, "Shoot, Son."

"You know that I haven't ever talked to you about anything private about the players. But something has come up that I don't know how to handle. I don't know if you will think it's any big deal, but I'm kind of worried about it. It has to do with Jesse and a girl."

The really sticky part was ahead of me, and I didn't know how I was going to bring up Maggie's reputation, and the fact that she was white and Jesse wasn't. Suddenly I felt ashamed of what I was doing. I didn't want to proceed. I was no better than anyone else who gloried in reporting in hushed tones the latest gossip. What I had thought were good intentions then looked petty and unworthy. The Coach saved me.

"Luke, I know what's on your mind."

"You do?" Boy, had the news flown! By the time a rumor had hit the faculty lounge, you knew that it had reached the end of the line. If Coach Levitson had already heard, the story must have circulated throughout the entire school.

"Jesse and I have already discussed it." he told me. "Yesterday."

I must have been under a rock to have only heard about it that day. To think that Coach and Jesse had previously discussed the issue was testimony to how out of touch I was with the latest developments.

"As a matter of fact, Luke, Jesse came to see me about the matter before school yesterday morning. I know that you weren't coming in here to be a tale-bearer, and that you were just trying to keep me abreast of the situation. I'm not telling you this so that you can try to stop the stories. Nobody can do that. But I think it may help you to understand if I tell you what Jesse told me. I'm not breaking his confidence by telling you, because he said that he was indifferent to what anybody said about him and would be happy to tell his side of it to anyone who asked for it. Which nobody has, I bet."

I sadly recognized that I was one of those who hadn't the nerve to ask Jesse anything, relying instead on my own speculations about what was going on and why.

"Jesse told me that on the day after the dressing room incident, when everybody was talking about what had happened, that only one student came up to him and expressed regret. She was the girl that you were going to tell me about. That is the only conversation she had with him, and the fact that he has been seen with her for the past couple of days is strictly because he has sought her out.

"There probably aren't 20 kids in this school who don't know of that girl's reputation. You may not know this, but she is a total outcast in this school. Jesse told me this, but I was aware of it. She has no friends. None. Now this is strictly confidential. She has attempted suicide twice. The most recent attempt was in August. Both times, as a matter of fact, have been in the summer. My guess is that the isolation she experiences every day at school is not as hard to bear as what she goes through during the vacation. She can always say hello to somebody at school, and there's always the hope, I suppose, that someone will befriend her. I imagine the loneliness of the summer months is too much for her sometimes.

"Anyway, as a student new to this school, Jesse probably heard about her position on the totem pole sooner or later. I do know that he is fully aware of her status. He also knows of the rumors that are circulating about the two of them since he's been seen with her. What he came to tell me was that she had done him the favor of speaking to him when none of the other students had, and that he was grateful to her for her kindness to him. He told me that he knew that some of the students and maybe even team members would resent him for what he was doing, but that he was going to do it anyway."

I don't know why Jesse's extraordinary doings still amazed me. I had seen enough of them to get accustomed to the idea that he was capable of one remarkable deed or word after another. But I was awed, nevertheless. Would I ever recognize that for Jesse, the extraordinary was the ordinary? Coach Levitson ended the period of revelation by telling me that Jesse was not acting out of pity.

"He says, and I believe him, that she is a good person, and that she has been put into a box, and that she hasn't been able to get out. He likes her and says she is his friend. The gossip mongers are going to have a field day with this, but I don't think he'll back down. Do you?"

Knowing what I did about Jesse, I knew he wouldn't, no matter what the price.

CHAPTER SEVENTEEN

The gymnasium at Cane Creek was the oldest and largest in the league. Our players swore it was longer than regulations allowed. It had been built when Cane Creek was prospering. Coal in the area had once been plentiful, and tons of tax money had been available for school construction. The town began to suffer economically when the coal ran short, but the residents still took good care of their mammoth building. The playing surface looked to have been made of a rare grade of wood not so easily paid for in the modern era. It was always glistening and reportedly never needed new paint for the court lines, so thoroughly was the original paint covered by multiple layers of varnish. Even though the floor looked glassy, the players reported that it offered excellent footing, with no dead spots. It was always a pleasure to play at Cane Creek, for reasons that went beyond the attractions of the old gym.

The people at Cane Creek were fanatics about basketball. Every time we played there, our fans found it hard to find a seat. The population of Cane Creek didn't actually amount to the 600 people who followed the Cougars. It was the outlying areas that provided much of the home team's support. Farmers still in their bib overalls were a common sight in the stands, and the enthusiasm which a Cougar crowd could generate was unmatched in the league.

I mentioned earlier that the Cougars were usually not very good. They and we often struggled with each other to avoid the bottom of the standings. Their lack of success over the years, however, had done little to diminish the support for the team. Every year was a new promise, and the fans continued to offer their loyalty to a team that seldom repaid it with many victories.

The junior varsity game had ended with the Anglers falling short by two points, and that put the home town fans in good spirits as the varsity game was about to begin. The seven juniors who made up the junior varsity group toweled themselves and accepted congratulations from the rest of the team for their effort. They weren't especially downcast, since they all knew they would play in the varsity game, the one that really counted.

Coach Levitson hadn't immediately followed the j.v. players to the dressing room. His delay caused some anxiety since we could hear the cheers for the Cougars when they had taken the court for their warm-up. We needed to get going!

When Coach entered, his face was flushed and he was highly agitated. He paced back and forth in front of us a few times, as if he was trying to decide what he wanted to say. When he stopped, he looked at the ceiling and then jammed his hands in his coat pockets and spoke: "Boys, the principal of Cane Creek has just reported to me that an anonymous caller has informed him that someone in the stands has a gun. The caller also said that the person intends to shoot Jesse."

We were all stunned. How could anyone make sense of it? At Cane Creek, where the people are always so friendly? My thought was that it was a horrible joke, until Coach Levitson said, "Mr. Porter, their principal, is fairly sure that, from the sound on the line, it was a long-distance call. The caller was a woman who was extremely upset. She may be related to the person who's reported to have the pistol. Mr. Porter is convinced that it's not a joke. He's called the sheriff's department, and three uniformed deputies are being sent at once. We're hopeful that if they're highly visible throughout the game, that no one will get hurt. Jesse, I'm sorry to have to tell you this, but we can't take any chances, so you won't be able to play tonight. I want you to stay in the dressing room. I've asked Mr. Abrams to stay here with you. I'm very sorry. Boys, we're going to skip our warm-up, and we won't go out on the floor until Mr. Porter tells me that the deputies have arrived."

Coach looked both confused and beaten. He was distressed and had no solution to the problem. It had him whipped. It was a season of silences. So many events had occurred that left us speechless. I guess I remember those periods of quiet as distinctly as anything about that year. In a matter of a few weeks, we had endured more of those excruciating moments when nobody knew what to say next, than in all of the years I had been with the team combined.

"Coach," Jesse said, "if it works tonight, it will work every night."

"What do you mean, Son?"

"If the threat keeps me off the team tonight, what's going to stop it from happening again? I think I ought to play."

Coach saw Jesse's point, as we all did. But what he was proposing was more than I knew Coach would allow.

"Jesse, we can't risk it. We just can't."

"It's not the first one, Coach."

Coach looked puzzled and asked Jesse once more what he was referring to.

"I've had two of those threats in the past two days. Or I should say my mother and I have. I got a call at home, and she got one at work. They both said about the same things. The man who called me said that I'd be shot after school yesterday if I was seen with a certain person at lunch. The call my mother got was late yesterday afternoon. The man said that I would be shot if I didn't stay home from school today. You can see that neither one of the threats was carried out. I think I ought to play."

Now my head was really spinning. Twice Jesse had challenged the threats. He was willing to test the third one. Coach was obviously at a loss for words. Like the rest of us, he couldn't comprehend what Jesse had been going through. When he finally spoke, it was weakly and in a way that implied that he was dealing with a situation entirely out of his control: "Did you call the Jewelton police?"

"Yes, sir. I spoke to Officer Smith about both of them."

"What did he say?"

"He told me that these threats usually follow a pattern. Ordinarily they're from people trying to get control over someone they don't like. He told me that they are meant to make the person who gets them change his pattern of living that the caller doesn't like."

"Didn't he tell you that they were serious? Didn't he say that these threats are sometimes carried out?"

Jesse looked completely calm. He and Coach could have been engaged in a conversation about what Jesse had done on his summer vacation for all the emotional effect it seemed to have on him.

"Yes, sir, he did tell me that. He told me that as the number of calls increased, if they were from the same caller, the likelihood was greater that he might do something. But this is only the third one, and you said yourself that it was from a woman."

"*Only* the third one!" A comment like that was what sometimes made me wonder if Jesse had normal human responses. If I had my life threatened even once, I'd jump on the next train out of town. But he was arguing the technicalities of who made the call. It was at that point that I gave up trying to figure him out. I swore then and there that I wouldn't waste another second of my life attempting to understand what made him tick.

I could see no weakening on Coach Levitson's part, but perhaps that was due to his state of confusion. "Son, the woman who made the call tonight might be the wife of the nut who called you before. She may know that he's gone off the deep end, and she may be trying to prevent him from acting. I can't let you go out there."

Jesse wasn't persuaded. "Coach," he countered, "I'll be OK. I'm more scared of what will happen if I start to run than if I don't. Please don't hold me out! If there really is someone out there with a gun, I think that I'm a lot safer in front of all those people than I was going to school by myself this morning."

Coach wasn't through with the debate. "He may not have been out there with a gun this morning. Maybe he just wanted to see if he could scare you. When you didn't stay home, it may have made him crazy. With what you've told me, I'm more convinced than ever that this is real."

The other players and I were like spectators at a tennis match, flip-flopping our heads as the verbal tennis ball hopped from one side of the net to the other.

Jesse took the Coach's last offering and sent it back. "Coach, one thing that you must understand is that this has to end somewhere. People like me have to face the fact that there are some people who are going to do everything they can to stop us. I've accepted that, and I'm asking you to accept it, too. If my mother doesn't ask me to stop, I don't think you should."

That was the winning point. Coach Levitson said nothing at first. The mention of Jesse's mother did it, I think, because Coach eventually said, "I'm opposed to it, Son, but I'm not the most important part of this decision. God help me if I'm making a mistake. I'll tell Mr. Porter that you're going to play."

While he was gone, 13 teen-aged boys sorted through their limited experience of life to find something that pertained to the crisis which a fourteenth boy was going through. Finding that experience lacking, we shuffled our feet, cleared our throats, got drinks of water, and became aware of the growing chant outside. The Cane Creek fans were demanding that the game get underway. The fact that we hadn't appeared was inexplicable to them, but they didn't care why we were delayed. They wanted us out there to play basketball. Coach came back and reported, "I've just had a devil of a time convincing Porter and the deputies of what we're about to do, but they finally gave in. Jesse, your mother can influence folks a long way from home." Our nervous laughter was occasioned by the realization that Coach Levitson had invoked Jesse's mother as his trump card in the discussion with the Cane Creek officials. Coach tried to regain the role as director of our basketball fortunes, but I knew that his mind wasn't going to be on the game any more than ours were. We were thinking about a maniac and his target.

Jesse played as if nothing had happened. The other Anglers played as if everything had happened. Phil dropped two passes. Johnny dribbled the ball off his foot when no one was guarding him and fell trying to get the ball, which rolled out of bounds. Tom missed two layups in the first quarter. Jude shot a free throw that hit no part of the goal at all. I'm certain that it was mystifying to the Cane Creek fans how we had beaten Apollo.

The second quarter was worse. We fell behind by 10 points. Half the crowd sat behind our bench and Cane Creek's. Where was he? Right behind us, or across the floor? Did he see the deputies? Why weren't the sheriff's men making themselves more conspicuous? When a bulb on the scoreboard popped slightly as it blew out, very few of the crowd seemed to notice, but all of us on the bench flinched. At the half, we were losing by 11.

Coach's halftime talk was one sentence: "If Jesse's got his head in the game, I think the rest of you should be able to do the same thing." We started a surge in the third period and caught up with four minutes to go in the game. Jesse was on the court the whole time, as Si was still not recovered from his leg injury. I hated it every time that Jesse came to a complete halt. During a free throw or a timeout, I would think, "Don't just stand there! Move around!" When he was in action I breathed easier, because his speed made him not only hard for the Cougars to keep up with, but all the harder for an unknown psychopath in the stands to get a bead on him.

Despite it all—the fear and apprehension and the bad case of nerves which they produced—we were able to beat Cane Creek. The Red crew was able to pull itself together enough to eke out the win. Jimmy Alpheson made two free throws at the end for a three-point victory. It wasn't very impressive to the people who had heard that Jewelton was better than usual, but I could vouch for the fact that the win had been our best of the year. Much relief and some happiness were evidenced by the players when they got back to the dressing room. It wasn't until several miles out of Cane Creek in our new bus that the tension evaporated fully.

For the next four weeks we heard nothing more about any incident like the one at Cane Creek. Coach told us one day at practice when Jesse was at home sick, that Officer Smith had been staying in touch with Jesse and his mother, and that they had received no more threats.

I list the following for a purpose: Roth, Lee Valley, Brown's Crossing, Salem, Tower Grove, Rhodenville, and Charter House. In the month that followed the Cane Creek game, we beat them all. It was a glorious ride through the first half of our league schedule. For the first time in its history, Jewelton had won 10 games in a row! We were flying high!

CHAPTER EIGHTEEN

The defeat of Charter House in our gym was the last game of 1960. As we began the new year, we were in first place. Charter House had beaten all the other teams in the conference and was only a game behind us. We had to play Charter House and Apollo at their gyms, but we had established ourselves as the team to beat.

The second part of our round-robin schedule would begin with the Apollo game and end with Charter House. If we could beat them both again, I was confident that we would take all the games in between and win the B-West title for the first time in a generation. One of Jewelton's most avid supporters was Walt Westlake, who had been an Angler player himself many years before. He provided us with the information from his personal records, showing we were on the school's longest win streak ever. The last Jewelton league championship had been in 1940. The team was also on the verge of getting a berth in the state tournament, since the top four teams from each of the B classifications received invitations. Mr. Westlake pointed out to me that it had been 11 years since the Anglers had even been in the tournament.

Our chance to go to the tournament looked like an almost-sure thing, and the league championship was a realistic hope. We had to play great basketball for the next six weeks, and the players were showing every sign that they could do it.

The second half of the season didn't start until the first week in January, and practice during the holidays was spirited. Players who started the season so divided had developed into a team remarkable for its harmony. They yelled encouragement to each other and razzed each other; they arrived early for practice and stayed late. They had adopted Coach's tactic of splitting into groups for free-throw and shooting contests—and this they did after practice ended. I was compelled on several occasions to turn off the gym lights to let them know they had to quit so I could go home. When Coach charged that they had gotten flabby from over-indulgence at the holiday feasts, he re-instituted sprints and laps as of old; the players responded good-naturedly to the drills and quipped to him that they thought he should use them more often. "It builds character, Coach." Pete said. "I think you mean 'characters,'" was Coach's reply.

It must have been close to seven o'clock one night, after I had been at the light switch to discourage the team from any more extra-curricular contests, that I finally got home from practice. My mother told me that Johnny had called and said that it was urgent that I call him back. When I did, he asked if I had heard the news about Jesse.

"Someone beat him up when he was on his way home from practice. He's hurt bad. He crawled to a house nearby and was taken from there to the hospital—by ambulance. From what I heard, he's in real bad shape."

Although I had thoughts about a medical career, I had admitted to myself on more than one occasion that my aversion to hospitals was going to be a problem for someone who wanted to be a doctor. As much as I feared the hospital, I told Johnny that we needed to go there right away. He said he'd be by to pick me up. I told my parents about what happened to Jesse, and they were horrified.

"Oh, Lord, I thought that was all over," Mom lamented. I had told her and Dad about the death threats, and they, like everyone else had known about the writing on the wall. "Do you think this has anything to do with Jesse's friendship with that girl?" my father asked. He didn't say "that girl" in any disparaging way; Dad just wasn't strong on remembering names.

"I don't know, but Jesse has stayed her friend, and that may be what's behind it. But the strange thing is that nobody at school has seemed to resent their friendship. I thought that everybody had gotten used to it, and that it didn't matter to anybody anymore. She and Jesse aren't isolated from the rest of the kids like they were at first. People have been friendly. I just don't think anybody at school could have done this."

By the time Johnny and I got to the hospital, all the others from the team were there, along with Coach Levitson, Mr. Abrams, and Jesse's mother. We all sat in the waiting room, and the conversation, what little there was of it, was barely audible. Jesse's mother was flanked by Coach and our principal, and each of them was holding one of her hands. She had tears in her eyes and on her cheeks, and the sight of her was so sad that I couldn't look more than once. Andy whispered to Johnny and me that Jesse was being operated on for internal injuries. Whoever beat him must have hit or kicked him in the stomach several times. Johnny and I had arrived about 7:30, and the word was that it would be after nine o'clock before the doctors would be through.

Officer Smith came about eight. He asked Mrs. Crosse if he could speak to her and the two men at her side, and they left the waiting room. When they had gone, the players began to fill each other in with what they had heard. Jesse had apparently been attacked as he walked on Dolor Street. He must have been dragged off into an alley, because the street was fairly heavy with traffic, and it wasn't likely that what happened took place in public. Matt Tachsman lived on Dolor. The people whose house Jesse made it to had called Matt right after they called the ambulance. Matt trembled when I asked him how Jesse looked.

"His face was horrible! He had blood everywhere, and dirt and gravel looked like they were ground into his cheeks and eyebrows." Matt was finding it difficult to repeat the story which he said he had already told Officer Smith. He added that Smith was on the scene before the ambulance got there and had asked Jesse if he knew who had beaten him. Matt repeated Jesse's statement that he knew it was two men, or big boys, but that he hadn't seen their faces.

Matt couldn't go on. With tears in his eyes, he went to the restroom. Pete leaned over to Johnny and said that Matt had been in the ambulance with Jesse and had seen Jesse starting to vomit blood. When Matt came back, I noticed that one leg of his trousers was darkly stained from hip to knee. Shortly, Mrs. Crosse, Coach, and Mr. Abrams returned, and we waited.

It was almost 9:30 before a doctor came in to the waiting room. The period of thinking the worst and hoping for the best was over. He revealed nothing of the outcome of the surgery by his look, and he asked Mrs. Crosse to follow him. By continuing to hold their hands tightly, it was apparent that she wanted Coach and Mr. Abrams to go with her, which they did. The length of time they were gone was agonizing. It doesn't take long to tell someone good news. We looked hopelessly at each other.

Then Coach Levitson came back alone. He was stony-faced. His voice quaked as he told us the report: "Boys, the operation is over. Jesse has had a very serious injury to his stomach which the doctors say they have successfully treated. But he may have lapsed into a coma. The doctors won't be certain about that until the anesthetic has worn off. Mr. Abrams and I are going to take Mrs. Crosse to stay with Mrs. Abrams, and then we will return. Mrs. Crosse has asked me to tell you how much it means to her that you have come, but that she wants you to go home, too. Mr. Abrams and I agree with her in every respect. Thank you for coming."

He left the waiting room, but no one made a move to follow him. Pete attempted to modify Coach's message by suggesting that the seniors would stay and the others should leave. Still no one left. And so we sat until Coach and Mr. Abrams came back in about 30 minutes. Neither of them showed any surprise that we were still there, but they were insistent that we should go. We reluctantly obeyed, with the assurance that they would keep us informed about Jesse's condition.

As we left the hospital lobby, we encountered the unexpected. The parking lot was jammed with students. They had been requested to stay there by a hospital official, who assured them that there was no room for them to wait in the hospital. What looked like three-quarters of the students in the school was waiting silently for word about Jesse's condition. The 13 of us approached them hesitantly. We had nothing to offer by way of good news. When the two groups confronted each other, there was silence.

In the front of the students was Maggie. She was sobbing, but she asked me, "Doc, what's happened?" The role of spokesman had fallen to me, and I knew that there was no avoiding it. I tried to be careful that I said nothing that I wasn't sure about. I realized that what I said could be mangled by the process of one person telling it to another. Everything I said, I said twice. I could tell that I wasn't telling them all they wanted to know, but I emphasized that my speculations were worthless. I could only report what Coach had told us. When it became clear that my news was neither good nor complete, a few went to their cars and left. Most stayed. I heard arrangements being made in the crowd to keep a constant watch. It became clear that the on-the-spot organizing was going to insure that at least 20 people would wait in the parking lot until some significant development took place. The voice in the crowd, which was directing the times of the vigil and who would be there and when, was John Mercer's. In a matter of minutes he had disbanded all but 20 students, setting times for the others to return for three-hour shifts. I wanted to thank him for his effort, but when I approached him, I saw that he probably wouldn't have wanted to be talked to at that moment. He had begun to cry.

On our way home, Johnny and I decided to join the students in the parking lot at five the next morning. Just five minutes before my alarm was scheduled to wake me, the jangling of the telephone did. It was Coach Levitson, calling from the hospital.

"Luke, we've got good news. Jesse has come out of the anesthetic just fine. The doctors say that he's woozy and a little out of his head, but he'll be as good as new in a few weeks. I wanted to call you now because I'm going home to bed, and I thought you could spread the news at daybreak, when I'll probably be sound asleep." I told the Coach that I would call all the players, starting at six o'clock. I asked him if he knew about the students waiting in the parking lot. He said he did, and that he would tell them the news, and that they should go home, too. I made 12 calls starting at six and disrupted many a household in the process, but everyone was excited by the news and thanked me for calling.

Jesse got out of the hospital a week later. He was reportedly making excellent progress, but I learned that the beating had hurt more than his body. Even though he received huge numbers of visitors, and flowers, and cards while he was hospitalized, none of it cheered him up. He was depressed and worried. One day, just before he was released, he and I were alone in the hospital room. From out of nowhere, related to nothing that we had been talking about, he said, "They're going to get me, Luke."

I didn't need an explanation. His dread was apparent, and I couldn't do much more than listen to him talk about it. Despite the fact that Officer Smith and, to a lesser extent, the others on the police force were working to find out who had beaten Jesse, there were no significant clues in the case. Jesse told me that the police were stumped, and speculated that they would never find out who did it. I had to respond to his dire prediction. "Jesse, I'm sure they're going to catch them," I said half-heartedly.

For the past few days his face had been returning to its normal size. It had been grotesquely swollen at first. He looked, except for some healing cuts, as he always had looked. But there was a difference in his eyes. They were empty of the confidence that I had become accustomed to seeing there. Dullness had replaced the sparkle, the life.

"I don't think so, Luke. I'm just going to have to face it."

I had no way to counter his pessimism. I just sat there, dumbly, sadly realizing that he sounded resigned to whatever happened. Beyond providing him with company, I was no help to him.

Then we heard surprising news about Jesse shortly after his release from the hospital. His doctors told him that he could rejoin the team if he could regain the weight he had lost during his time of convalescence. For a while he had eaten little or nothing, and he lost several pounds. The doctors put his possible date of return to the team at about mid-February, some six weeks after he had been beaten.

That good news, and it was only potentially good, was about all that we had as far as basketball was concerned. The Apollo game had come only two days after Jesse was attacked, and the Suns trounced us at their place, even though Pete had fired up the team before the game by asking them to dedicate it to Jesse. What nobody told Jesse was that the 18-point loss had been dedicated to him.

We did beat Cane Creek for the second time, but lost to Roth, Lee Valley, and Brown's Crossing before we won again. The guys were making a mighty effort, but it was evident that without Jesse we weren't much better than average. The last three games in the conference were also losses, the worst being the finale at Charter House. The Demons were even rougher on us than Apollo had been, and they ended their season as champs of the league with a 17-1 record. Our upset of them was their only loss, and they made us pay for that blot on their otherwise perfect season by clobbering us, 74-49.

We finished the year with 12 wins and six losses in B-West, much better than anyone could have anticipated at the beginning of the season, but disheartening when we thought about what we had been hoping for. We did finish fourth in the conference and got a spot in the state tournament, but with Jesse's return doubtful, and the team's spirit at low ebb, we tried to think positively about what progress we had made and the prospects for next year.

CHAPTER NINETEEN

Even though our season ended on a sour note, I began to get excited about playing in the state tournament—held, as usual, in Jericho, on the state's eastern edge, about 175 miles from Jewelton. Jericho was the largest town, or city, which was in the class B tournament. Many of us, including me, were looking forward to our first trip there.

We were certainly going to be strangers. The Anglers hadn't sent a team to the tournament since the 1940s, and it was unlikely that many people in Jericho had ever heard of our little town on the other side of the state. Arrangements for going to a state tournament are made on a day-to-day basis. One loss, and you're out—out of the hotel room, out of town, and out on the road home, full of regret that you didn't win just one more game so you could stay one more day. We had a week to get ready for our trip. Reservations were made for the Hotel Noble, for only one night, with the understanding that it could be for as many as four nights for a team which could go all the way to the finals. The hotel was going to be overrun with basketball players and their fans. Fifteen teams, every team in the tournament except Jericho's, would make the Noble their headquarters for the week. I was looking forward to it, except the anticipated drive of four hours in Coach Levitson's creeping style. Since our wreck in the earlier part of the year, he had eased back on the throttle even more. We felt that we were lagging behind everybody—snail included.

I suppose that all of Jewelton's supporters had been disappointed by our downturn at the end of league play, but enthusiasm picked up noticeably as the team prepared for the tourney. Spirits dampened, however, when we learned our first opponent would be Columbia, champions of B-North. The draw of Columbia, or a team as good as they were, wasn't unexpected. We knew that whoever we played would be extremely tough. The team pairings for the tournament was designed to bring the strongest teams in each of the four divisions together in the semi-finals. The winners of each division would play the fourth-place team from another conference, with second-place finishers playing those who came in third. Only an upset could prevent the strongest teams from playing each other when it got down to four teams. It was a fair arrangement, but I would have liked it better if the Anglers hadn't ended up fourth.

"Clobber Columbia!" and "Demote the Captains!" typified the signs I saw plastered all over school. Students were starting to catch state-tournament fever. Unfortunately, very few of them would get to see Jewelton play, because our game was scheduled for a Wednesday night, and nobody would be excused from school the following day with the alibi of having been to the game the night before; even Mr. Abrams, the principal, was planning to drive back after the game so he would be at school on Thursday.

For the first time in six weeks, Jesse participated in practice. It was five days before the game with Columbia. While he was healing, he had come to every practice and had attended every game. He volunteered his services to me as my assistant, and even though I felt goofy having our best player as my underling, I was glad to have his help. I was even gladder to see his state of mind improve as time passed. He was down like the rest of us when the team lost, as it did quite often in those weeks, but his fatalistic attitude seemed to be undergoing a change. He wasn't subject to periods of depression, at least none that I could detect. Time did seem to be healing all his wounds. One project that Coach Levitson had given me was to encourage Jesse to eat. Coach weighed Jesse in his office a couple of days after he had been released from the hospital, and the scales showed 97 pounds. Jesse didn't act startled by the reading, but Coach collared me later, and said, cryptically, "Candy bars."

Interpretation? I was to carry them with me every day at practice and offer them to Jesse at every opportunity. Coach told me that Jesse's mother was concerned by his weight loss and had provided Coach with a box of Jesse's favorite candy bars. Mrs. Crosse said that she had been unable to convince Jesse to eat more. She had agreed with Coach that Jesse might take food if offered by another student, and that turned out to be me. The only catch: Coach wanted me to make the situation seem natural by eating a bar myself, and unfortunately I hated the concoction known as Zero, which was Jesse's bar of choice. The first time I offered him one, he looked suspiciously at me and said, "Where did you get that, as if I didn't know?" I saw no reason to lie, so I said that it came from Coach, who had gotten it from Jesse's mother. He laughed heartily at the setup, and asked whether I liked the bar I was gnawing on. I told him I hated it. He chuckled at the absurdity of it, and told me that he would make everybody happy by eating one or two each day, and that there was no need for me to join him.

"But, Doc, I think the medical association would wonder about the wisdom of your prescription of a Zero for your patient. I think they'd find you guilty of malpractice."

By the time he rejoined practice, Jesse had gained six pounds, but he was weak and, though I would have never have thought it possible four months earlier, out of shape. It was a good thing that Si had long since returned from his injury, because Jesse was in no condition to play an entire game. He had lost that inexhaustible source of energy that he once had, and his speed was down several notches. His timing on passes was off, and his teammates at first didn't seem to understand. They looked at him in doubt when he was unable to do what he'd done before. "What's wrong with you?" they seemed to be saying. I only had to remember the sight of him dressing before practice to find it easy to understand. He had hastily yanked off his shirt and pulled on his practice jersey, with his back turned to all in the room but me. I was taping Jude's ankle and just happened to look in Jesse's direction at that instant. There wasn't a big scar on his stomach—there were two, one perpendicular to the other. The scars looked reasonably well healed to my untrained eye, but the sight of them made me look away; they were ugly. I was thinking about becoming a doctor? When the sight of a person who was on the mend gave me the willies? Maybe it made a difference that I knew and admired the person and couldn't forget what he had been through that produced those marks on his body.

At the last practice, Coach Levitson told the team about Columbia. "Uncommonly tall," was his curt description. He instructed the players that the only way to offset that height advantage was to "run all night long." He doubted the stamina of their two biggest players, who were both about 6'5". "We won't get many rebounds of any shots that we miss early in the game, so let's not miss any. If you must miss a shot or two, save that for the second half, when they're going to be tired." He was talking so confidently that I began to believe his plan might work. Then I recalled his comment to me in September about a coach's need to boost morale, and I wondered if he himself had confidence in what he was saying.

"You're going to have to fight like mad for rebounds at their end of the court. We can't afford to let their big boys play catch under the goal until one of them finally makes a shot. I guess that just about does it, boys. Except for one last thing. You know I've been here a long time. I've had a lot of teams, and lots of players. I want to tell you something that I've never said to any team. I've had better players before, and I don't say that to hurt your feelings; I'm just telling you the truth. But the other side of that coin is that I've never had a better team. You've heard me talk enough about 'the team' to know what I'm telling you. No matter how we do over at Jericho, this team has been my best. Now, be sure you bring your suitcases to school tomorrow and remind your parents that we'll be leaving at noon and the game is at 8:30. Go shoot your free throws and get a good night's rest."

Ignoring his last sentence, the players fastened on his words of praise. They all knew that early in his career, Coach Levitson had three or four teams that had been excellent; one of them even made it to the semi-finals of the tournament. Yet he had told us that this team was his best! The guys shot their free throws quickly and with little to say to each other. They were proud.

The bus ride to Jericho wasn't nearly as pokey as I had thought it would be. That's because I slept about three-quarters of the way. Most everybody else seemed to have done the same. I woke up when we were already in Jericho, and I began to contrast its size and bustle with Jewelton's. I knew all the clichés about country boys being dazzled by the big city, and I had been determined to be blasé about whatever Jericho had to offer. But my resolution not to be overwhelmed went out the window with my sighting of a 20-story building and a low-slung modern structure with the word "Museum" on it. What struck me as noteworthy was how interested we on the bus were in the place and people of Jericho, and how totally indifferent they were to us. While we gawked at them and their environment, the people of Jericho didn't give us a second look. "That's the city," I thought, "in a big hurry and with no time to notice a busload of hicks." I was a little stung by their ignoring of us and wished that we could do something to get their attention. An upset of Columbia would do it.

When we got to the hotel, we were shocked to hear that Charter House had been upset in overtime in the first game of the day. Walnut Ridge beat them by a point. We had mixed reactions to the news. It did encourage us to think that a fourth-place team could beat a first-place team, which was our objective that night; but it also made us question the caliber of play in our conference, if our league champion couldn't defeat the fourth team in B-North. It was an omen we could interpret as either good or bad.

The Hotel Noble was a lot older and less fancy than I thought it would be. It was a brown brick building that didn't begin to compare in altitude with some of Jericho's newest, and the rooms were supplied with well-worn furniture. There were four of us to a room. Jesse and Phil were to room with

Coach and Mr. Abrams. Coach explained that as the two youngest, they had to forfeit the pleasure of being housed with the other players. We all groaned at the news of their fate, and kidded them about having two babysitters. Phil and Jesse took the kidding in stride, but I thought later that perhaps the adults might be keeping an eye on Jesse, considering all that had already happened.

I learned much later that Coach had problems with the hotel when he pre-registered us by phone. The hotel policy, the manager informed him, was to prohibit Negroes from staying there. Coach then called an old college buddy of his, the vice president of the state High School Athletic Association. A call from him informed the hotel manager that a number of the teams had Negro players, so the association might have to encourage all 15 teams to find another hotel for the four-day tourney. Seeing the possibility of thousands of dollars disappear, the hotel manager relented. When Coach told me that story, I've got to say I was proud of the High School Athletic Association, or at least that official, for taking such quick and positive action.

Coach told us all to get some rest before our 5:30 supper, although the sleep on the bus had provided more rest than the average teenager needed during the day. My roommates were Pete, Johnny, and Tom. We spent the hour and a half before the meal testing the bed and the plumbing, inspecting our window views of Jericho, and watching television. "You suppose every room in this hotel has a TV, or did we just hit it lucky to get one?" Tom asked. I, who considered myself wise to the ways of the world, assured him that it was standard equipment in all rooms.

As we were going to supper, we saw the happy fans of Horizon coming back to the hotel. We found out that Horizon had dumped Lee Valley, making it the second team from our conference to lose. It was a disastrous day so far for teams from our part of the state. It was food for further thought, but we concerned ourselves first with food for the body.

We ate what we assumed was the traditional "pre-game meal" that we had heard and read about. Since it was the first time we had ever engaged in one, we had no way of knowing if enormous servings of lima beans and small portions of meat, which is what we were provided with in the hotel dining room, were thought to be especially conducive to improved athletic performance. I made a mental note to ask Mr. Pearson, Jewelton's biology teacher, what benefits lima beans offered basketball players.

After we ate, we went back to our rooms and gathered up all we'd need for the game. It was a short drive to Jericho's field house. You note that I did not call it a gym. Affixed to its wall were metal letters that proclaimed it to be the Josh Nunn Field House. It was new, and it was huge. It had a swimming pool. It had seats for more fans than I thought could ever be interested in a high school basketball game. It was definitely a field house.

When we entered, there were hundreds of people in the bleachers, and yet hundreds of vacant seats. First-round games didn't draw too well, I gathered. As I looked at the scoreboard to check the totals of the game in progress, I was much impressed by two rectangular boards, the same height as the scoreboard, on which had been placed the names and numbers of each player. Next to each name was a row of tiny red lights which indicated the number of fouls each player had committed. Everything was up-to-date in Jericho!

We had arrived at the half of Apollo's first-round game. Apollo was second in our league, and was up against the third-place team from the same conference as Columbia. Bad news! Apollo was getting waxed, 32-18, by a team that was only third best in the B- North conference. What did that tell us about Columbia?

That score, along with the others involving the teams from our conference, unnerved everybody. We watched the first five minutes of the third period before heading to get dressed, and experienced the odd sensation of rooting for the team that had been a nemesis of ours for so many years. I amazed myself by cheering when the pugnacious Morris swished a long jump shot. The team from Needham was pouring it on Apollo, however, and as we went to the locker room, Hansen had fouled out, and the Suns trailed by 20. It looked like a day to forget for the B-West league.

I taped ankles and listened to sounds of the crowd outside. The cheering was subdued, indication enough that Apollo wasn't making a big comeback. The players were pensive, as the obligation to avoid a B-West whitewash was only minutes away. Coach Levitson was chipper, though. He wandered around from player to player, inquiring about how each one felt, and was showing no sign of the burden which had been placed on us.

Everybody was ready. The Apollo game was over, with the predictable result. Coach stood before us and smiled. "Boys, I've got great news. This is a game we're going to win! I was pretty sure of it, but now I'm convinced. One of our players, I won't say which, had a dream the night before the first Apollo game. He dreamed that we would win, and he dreamed the exact score. He has informed me that he dreamed about this game last night, and that we emerged as the winners. He didn't know the score, but it was a three-point victory. I have no doubt that he is correct. So go out there and get that win!"

As the team churned for the dressing room door, I again questioned Coach's tactics. It came to someone in a dream? Was he serious? Who was our dream boy, anyway? When Jesse passed me on the way out, with a sheepish grin, I thought I knew.

CHAPTER TWENTY

The Anglers took the court for their warm-up. The few fans from Jewelton clapped and cheered, but canyon-like Nunn Field House swallowed the sound. Columbia's entry, however, was greeted by a blast of approval from the stands which now had almost filled. Columbia was fewer than 100 miles from Jericho, and its supporters were legion. It amounted to the home-court advantage for the Captains.

Coach Levitson had said they were "uncommonly tall," but I would have described them as "out-of-this-world huge." If they had a player under six feet, he must have been hiding in the dressing room, humiliated by his lack of stature compared to his towering teammates. I closely observed the Columbia drills and concluded that they were by far the slickest looking outfit I had ever seen in a warm-up. They ran their drills with speed and efficiency. No missed layups, no sloppy passes, almost every shot a successful one. I noted that they didn't bother with many practice shots from long range. They obviously planned to do most of their scoring near the goal. I didn't like what I saw.

"Remember," Coach was instructing the White team just before the tip-off, "we've got to run them hard in the first half. If the break isn't there, I want you to make them work on defense. We've got to wear them down." The five starters burst from the huddle with a shout and went out to shake hands with what proved to be a taller opponent at every position.

The tap was Columbia's, and their point guard was at least five inches taller than Si, who was glued to him. How much more would he loom over Jesse when the second quarter got under way! Coach Levitson never believed in zone defense, where a player guards a portion of the court rather than a specific man. Time and again he stressed that such a defense diminished responsibility. He liked the idea that a defensive man was held accountable for the deeds of the man he was guarding. He thought it evoked more effort and pride than the zone. So each of our short guys had to struggle with the Columbia height advantage on a one-on-one basis. I suspected that a lot of the spectators were surprised to see that we weren't using the zone, but I knew that Coach wouldn't resort to it, no matter what.

Columbia's first offensive play made me sick. One of their largest bodies tried a shot and missed, but they rebounded and tried again. Once more the shot was off the rim, but they out-reached us for that rebound too! It was just what Coach said we couldn't allow: They were playing catch. On the fourth attempt, the ball curled around the hoop twice and finally fell through. Their shooting percentage was 25%, but they were winning.

Si got our offense rolling, and I was proud of the discipline that the Anglers showed. They restrained the urge to catch up right away, and they put into effect Coach's tactic of making the Captains chase us a great deal before we shot. It didn't take long for our patient offense to get on the nerves of the Columbia fans. They began booing when the Anglers had passed and dribbled the ball for over a minute without taking a shot. With the disapproval raining on them, the White unit made me even prouder. They didn't crack under the cacophony. Eventually, Phil popped open close to the goal and sank his shot, following a nifty pass from Jude. We were tied.

I thought it was odd that Columbia's coach called timeout. When Columbia scored again after three shots, I understood what the timeout was for. Columbia had abandoned its man-to-man defense for the zone. Their coach realized what our offense was doing. He could see that his players would get worn out if they had to pursue our faster players all night. The zone was less tiring for the defense, but it was also easier for us to make the many passes that Coach's offense called for. Our second time on offense enraged the Columbia crowd. We held the ball for over two minutes, and I counted our passes. There were 35 of them before Phil took his, and our team's, second shot. The ball rolled off the rim, but somehow Tom had slipped between the Captains' defenders to tip it in. The first quarter was half over, and only eight points had been scored. At that rate, the winner would score fewer than 40 points. So far, the game was definitely being played in a style to our advantage.

When the quarter ended, with Columbia leading 10-8, I looked over the statistics I had acquired for the first eight minutes. Columbia had shot 21 times and had made five. We were four for six. The White crew had admirably held its own, and the guys had almost perfectly lived up to Coach's admonition that they not miss any shots in the first half.

Jesse stole the ball from the Columbia guard, whose name was Wright.

Wright had committed the error of being too nonchalant in the encounter with such a little opponent. It was a mistake I had seen many a player make when first being guarded by Jesse. Jesse wasn't able to generate a fast break after his steal, so he slowed things down and began again to test the Captains' patience. The Red five had found the first quarter very instructive. They weren't about to hurry their shot, because they knew that if they missed, the rebound would likely be Columbia's. I lost track of the number of passes. The players who are behind must attempt to score. They can't freeze the ball if they are trailing. We weren't freezing it—we just weren't going to shoot until we could be reasonably sure of making it. Some of Columbia's backers were getting apoplectic at our style of play. Their booing had changed to insult. The invective was non-stop. They were outraged that the nobodies from some place called Jewelton were keeping the vaunted Columbia offense from showing its stuff. How was it going to look in the papers if they beat the fourth-place team from the West 30-20?

With three minutes left in the quarter, we still had not shot. "Pathetic" and "a travesty" and "chickens" were the few civil comments that were being directed at our team. But the Reds held firm. No good shot meant no shot at all. The Captains undoubtedly were getting very tired of the process themselves, but they seemed determined not to foul or do anything else indicating we were getting to them. At about the two-minute mark Jesse surprised everyone by driving hard to the goal. It was our first real threat in over five minutes. I was looking for the man he would pass to. I had learned that when Jesse went helter-skelter for what looked like a shot, he was actually setting up someone else. But I didn't see his intended target. Since I was watching our other four players, I missed seeing Jesse's shot. The pandemonium on our bench alerted me to the fact that we were tied, and Matt filled me in with the details of Jesse's basket. "He went right up and passed that big guy just like the guy was sleep-walking," Matt hollered.

Columbia was forced to be very careful with its shot selection, because the Anglers had proved to them that they weren't going to get many opportunities to score. They missed again, and Pete practically deflated the ball, so emphatically did he grab the rebound. Our offense went to its by-now predictable pattern, and although we missed the shot as time expired, we had won the first half as far as I was concerned, even though the score was 10-10.

On the way to the locker room I passed the long table at courtside and heard a radio announcer, broadcasting to parts unknown, say, "It's not the easiest game to announce, folks, but who could have predicted that the Columbia powerhouse would have only ten points at halftime?" In the dressing room, Coach pointed out that sometimes a game takes an unpredictable turn on its own, and that we were involved in such a game. "Obviously we didn't plan it quite this way, boys, but I think that we should continue to take what the game gives us. Unless Columbia makes some drastic change, I say that we keep doing what we've been doing."

The players were unanimous in their approval of the decision. Coach added a final comment before they returned to the game: "Remember that the other day I said you could save your misses until the second half? Having given it further consideration, I don't think it would be a good idea to miss any at all if you can help it." Laughing and charged up, they took to the floor and were met with merciless booing. The Columbia bleacherites were standing and screaming at them. It wasn't pleasant. There was more to it than just disapproval—it was hostility, and it made me nervous.

Columbia didn't change its tactics. The Captains scored shortly after winning the tip, and fell back into their zone. But it just wasn't able to put enough pressure on the White five to force them to shoot. Si was inspired in his selection of passes, and although they ganged up on him a couple of times to try to get the ball, he always managed to escape with a dribble or a pass. Tom hit a short shot with five minutes left. Tied at 12! The Captains blew their next try, bringing a scramble for the ball, which Phil came up with. The Anglers withstood the crowd's verbal assaults and the Captains' defense. As the quarter came to a close, Tom was caught in the corner with the ball and two of Columbia's defenders on him. He had no shot, so he held the ball as time ran out.

I thought the place was going to be the scene of mass hysteria. When Tom turned down a pointless attempt to score, the anger quotient seemed to double. It was almost impossible to hear Coach in the huddle before the last quarter, so high was the volume of booing. He was the picture of serenity, however. Impervious to the clamor, he spoke loudly but calmly. "I think they may go to a man-to-man this quarter. Be ready to jump on them if they do. Even with using the zone, they're tuckered out, so take advantage of it." The Red team, Jesse, Pete, Andy, Bart, and Jimmy, with Tradeau and Jim Wirges as their substitutes, had eight minutes to try to surpass the Captains' best efforts by only one point.

Columbia broke my heart again when they were able to get four shots on their first possession. The first three weren't so upsetting, but the fourth went in. Coach Levitson hit the nail on the head about their defense. They were going to force the issue by dropping the zone. Jesse was too quick for Wright, however, and he sped around him to the goal. As the twin towers of Columbia converged on him, Jesse whipped a no-look pass to Pete for a ridiculously wide-open basket. Columbia hadn't figured out how to handle us yet. Still tied.

The tempo of the game returned to something approaching normal, although the Anglers were still very conservative about their shots. With two minutes to go, and the score an improbable 20-20, Jim Wirges, fresh into the game for Andy, committed a foul as one of their giants was trying a close-in shot. It was a good foul, for it prevented a certain score. It turned out even better when the lanky Captain missed both free throws. Pete rebounded, and coach called timeout.

"Boys, I think we'd better go for the last shot," he told them. "I don't want to let them have it again if we can help it. The folks in the stands are going to get pretty loud when they figure out what we're up to, so close your ears and keep your brains in gear. I'm not going to call another timeout. They'll be expecting one at about 10 seconds if we hold it that long. So when it gets down to 10, just keep the offense going and get a shot with two or three seconds to go. If we miss that shot, we'll just tip it in and call it a day."

The crowd did begin to roar again as it became evident that the Anglers were going to hold the ball for one last shot. Columbia's defense was back to the zone. They weren't as likely to foul in that defense, making it probable that our last try, if we could get it, would have to be a long shot. My nerves were in shreds as the seconds ticked away. I was going numb. With less than a minute to go, Tradeau almost threw the ball away, but Pete jumped out of bounds with the ball and hurled it back onto the court to Jesse.

The last 30 seconds were agony. The din was impossible to believe. Some of the Columbia contingent was imploring its five to get the ball, while others concentrated on distracting the Anglers. Fifteen seconds to go. If coach was right, the Captains might be startled that we didn't soon call time out to set up a play. Nine seconds. Pete had the ball at the free-throw line, but had no chance to shoot. It was too early, anyway. He passed to Jesse. Jesse dribbled at the top of the keyhole, 20 feet from the basket. Too far for him. The players became a blur.

Five seconds to go—time to get a shot! Jesse began to back away from the goal! He was more than 25 feet away as he launched the ball. The timing was perfect, but the length of the shot wasn't. A mass of bodies swarmed under the goal, all eyes looking for a rebound. Then I realized Jesse had launched no shot at all. While all the others were watching the rim for the bounce, Pete was watching Jesse's lofted pass. Pete went up in the air before anyone else. He caught the ball and banked it before he came down. One of Columbia's tall ones saw what was happening and swatted at Pete's hands. A foul! And a basket!

With one second to go, Pete made his free throw. Columbia's full-court try fell far short. 23-20. Final. The dreamer's vision had come true.

CHAPTER TWENTY-ONE

Jericho's morning newspaper featured the two upsets of the first round: Walnut Ridge's win over Charter House and our defeat of Columbia. I thought the reporter who covered our game must have been among those who were screaming at our players; he didn't like what he had seen us do to Columbia. He described our offense as "a boring slow-down, displeasing to the fans who have come to see basketball, not catch, being played." He also called Jesse's last pass "an anemic shot which was fortunate enough to fall into Barjon's hands." The greatest win in recent Jewelton history was being demeaned for its style and its reliance on luck. Maybe we were lucky, but was that a fault? It took a little of the luster off the victory to see it treated as a fluke, but we were still in Jericho, and Columbia's players were packing their suitcases; those were the facts, whether the writer liked them or not.

Our game on Thursday was at 5:30, and we would be playing Drake Central. Drake was from the South conference and had won its first game by eight points. We had a team meeting at 11 that morning. Coach Levitson told us Drake was not as big as Columbia, but they were a lot faster. He reported that in their first win they had made 60% of their shots and nine of 10 free throws. "They seem to really have an eye for the basket, boys, so we're going to have to play extra hard on defense." Drake promised to be a formidable opponent. There was no point in expecting any state tournament game to be easy.

We had a few hours to kill before the game, so we went to a movie. We were leery of the odd title, "The Mouse That Roared," but it was a funny show about a tiny country that planned to invade the United States. Its logic was that when it lost the "war" to the U.S., as the defeated country it could demand foreign aid, and thereby get a shot in the arm to its failing economy. Through a series of goof-ups, the little nation almost won the war. In the end though, everything worked out as planned, and defeat actually became victory, as the hoped-for results came to pass. Even though the movie was a comedy, I was provoked to think that if defeat could turn into victory, couldn't victory also become a defeat? I was thinking of what I considered the unfair treatment of the Anglers by the Jericho sports writer. We certainly got very little credit for our upset victory over Columbia. The fans were down on us; the newspaper portrayed us as dull and lucky to win on a freak play, and I withdrew my prediction that a defeat of Columbia would get us some respect in Jericho.

No dose of lima beans greeted us before the game on Thursday. Since we played at 5:30, we wouldn't eat supper until after the game, a meal that would feature hamburgers at a little restaurant, rather than a fancier meal in the hotel dining room. We got to Nunn Field House as the day's first game, Horizon versus Satterfield, was starting the second half. Horizon, the conquerors of Lee Valley, looked likely to make it to the semi-finals. They were winning by 12 points.

Although we were hoping that we'd have more fans than the night before, with the game tipping off so early, we doubted that many people from Jewelton would be able to make it. At the warm-up, our rooting section looked to be about 20—perhaps a 10th of the crowd backing Drake. Once again we would have to play without that uplifting and inspiring force that a mass of avid supporters could provide. Coach commented on the phenomenon of crowd support, perhaps sensing our disappointment in scarcity of friendly faces in the bleachers.

"Boys, it's nice to have all the folks yelling for you. But the crowd can't win it for you. The Columbia players found that out last night, if they didn't already know it. You haven't lived long enough to make the comparisons that I can. In my 35 years of being associated with basketball as a player and a coach, I never saw a team win under circumstances as unfavorable as those you had to face last night. I want you to consider the win against Columbia as I do: a game that we had absolutely no business winning—and that we won, nevertheless. No team I've ever coached amazed me as much as this one did last night. The 'dogs of war,' as Shakespeare called them, were on the loose last night in this gym, and you beat them. So try not to worry about the numbers out there except the ones on the scoreboard. You can rely on each other to get the job done. Let's do it again tonight!"

Perhaps it was the stinging rebuke contained in the paper that did it. Maybe it was the Drake crowd booing them when they took the court. Maybe it was Coach's praise. Whatever it was, the Anglers played with an energy unmatched by any that season. They were aggressive on defense without getting into foul trouble. They passed the ball all over the court without throwing it away. They ran the fast break time after time against players who were supposed to be their equals in speed. I almost felt sorry for Drake. By the end of the first quarter it was no contest. The excellent shooting of the Spartans had deserted them. We were ahead by 15 at the half and 22 by the start of the fourth quarter. Ordinarily, a coach would insert little-used substitutes to mop up such a one-sided game, but we really didn't have any subs of that kind. All of our players were accustomed to game conditions, and even though Tradeau and Jim Wirges played the last eight minutes for Jesse and Bart, there was little drop-off in the level of play. We won 68-40, and the score would have been worse, except that Coach called a timeout and demanded that the Reds make at least 10 passes before taking a shot. The law was in effect for the game's last six minutes, but our shooters were enjoying a banner night, exemplified by the fact that they made seven of nine shots in the fourth period, and the hapless Drake team was soundly whipped.

We downed record numbers of hamburgers, much to the satisfaction of the restaurant owner who must have concluded that winning teams eat lots more than losing ones. Then we returned to the hotel to savor the fact that we had made it to the semi-final game against Horizon. No team from Jewelton had ever done better! I could hardly wait for the morning paper. We had played an almost flawless game, and the grumpy reporter would have to give us our due.

"Jewelton took no mercy on the fatigued Spartans in the last quarter. Coach Mo Levitson's charges played cat-and-mouse with the ball for the last minutes and humbled the hustling Drake five by giving them no chance to catch up."

That was the final paragraph of the next day's story about the game. It was also the final straw! Who was this idiot who wrote under the name of M.A. Donner? Instead of recognizing that Coach took pity on Drake, he accused us of rubbing it in. We were pictured as merciless, and the Drake players were described as weary but doggedly trying to catch up. Speaking of catching up, where did Mr. Donner get the notion that we were obliged in some way to let Drake catch us? I took momentary satisfaction in observing that the writer's initials spelled out "mad," which I thought he was indeed, but it was only a fleeting relief from the effect on me of his poison pen.

Friday's semi-final games were ours with Horizon at 7 p.m. and Jericho's against Hamilton at 9 p.m. I was grateful for our chance to play in the first game, because the day dragged. We went out on a bus tour of Jericho before lunch, but I was so angry about the Jericho paper's treatment of us that I was determined to find nothing redeeming about the whole town. My spite worked. Sights that I would have enjoyed had we been getting a fair shake in the press I found tacky or flawed in one way or another. It was a fault-finding tour as far as I was concerned, and it only soured my mood further. And the time passed in slow motion. Following lunch, the players were told to get at least two hours of rest—sleep if possible. Coach made it clear that he wanted no bull sessions or departures from the rooms. We settled down for a long afternoon.

The crawling afternoon was to end with a team meeting at four o'clock. It would be Coach's scouting report of Horizon. We were starting to perk up as game time approached. As we entered the room off the lobby that the hotel provided us for our chalk-talk, I noticed Matt excitedly talking in low tones to Pete. Pete's face turned pale and he looked hurriedly about the room. A stern Coach Levitson stormed in. He started the meeting before all the players had even showed up. Then I found out why. Coach reported that three of our players had been caught outside their room during the rest period. He didn't have to name them. The Alphesons and Tradeau were not in attendance. Coach said that they were suspended for that night's game. He gave no further details and began his report about Horizon. I hoped the players were able to follow what he was saying, because I wasn't. Tradeau's loss wasn't significant, but the Alphesons each held a starting position on the White and Red teams. Their presence would be greatly missed. At the end of the meeting, Coach announced that Matt would take Jude Alpheson's place on the White team, and Jim Wirges would substitute for Jimmy. That was it. Two of our best players were banished from the biggest game of their lives.

Coach left abruptly, leaving 10 shocked players and me to try to make sense of what had happened. Matt was the roommate of the three. He said that they had sneaked out of the room to meet some cheerleaders from Horizon. He had argued with them about it, but they were determined to show up for the rendezvous in the hotel coffee shop. Matt didn't know who had caught them, or how, but we knew that Coach interpreted their activities as violations of his Ten Points, with no hope that he would change his mind.

Pete and I went back with Matt to his room, thinking we might find the suspended players there. They were. Their reaction was not uniform. The Alphesons were crushed—they had each been crying. Tradeau, on the other hand, was angry. He was in total rebellion against Coach Levitson for what he considered harsh treatment of a minor violation.

"We were resting," he argued. "We were just sitting and talking, and then Levitson appears out of nowhere and orders us up to his room. He made us look like jerks in front of those girls and then pulled his tough-guy act on us when he got us upstairs. He gets a big thrill out of pushing people around."

Tradeau's self-defense evoked no response from the rest of us. We tried to console the Alphesons, but Jimmy was certain that he had ruined his opportunity to play in his last high school game ever. Johnny took exception to Jimmy's self-pity and pointed out to him that what he was saying amounted to a prediction that Horizon would beat us. Jimmy seemed to snap out of it then, and said, "I'm sorry guys. The reason Coach treated us like jerks is that we are jerks. Do me a gigantic favor and beat Horizon so I don't end my basketball career as a jerk. Give me a chance to play tomorrow night." Jude was also contrite and wished Pete and Johnny well, but Tradeau was still alternating between snarling and mewling as we left. He wasn't resigned at all to his fate.

We got to the field house about 6:30. And what a treat we had in store! Fans from Jewelton were waiting for us—probably 200 of them. They had found out from Coach Levitson where he would park the bus, and they were massed in the parking lot. They were wild, waving signs and bobbing red-and-white pom-poms and hollering, "Anglers! Anglers!" I felt warmth at the base of my neck spreading into the back of my head. I realized that I was just about to cry—in gratitude, I guess. I checked myself and exchanged disbelieving looks with Pete and Johnny. When we got off the bus, the yelling increased, though I didn't think it possible. How nice to know that our families and friends were there, in what had come to feel like a very hostile environment!

As we went into the field house, I wondered what all those people were going to do for an hour before the game. It turned out that they'd raise the roof. They shouted in unison with the cheerleaders; they broke into spontaneous rounds of clapping and stomping. I hoped that they would have something left for the game.

I shouldn't have underestimated our 200. They drowned out the fans from Horizon, who were at least as many as they. Throughout the pre-game drills they bellowed and roared. They were incredible! For the first time in the tournament, our players warmed up with smiles on their faces. Once the game began, our rooters pulled out all the stops. When we won the tip-off, another first for us in the tournament, they howled and treated Tom's deed as if it were the winning basket.

Horizon was rugged, but not rugged enough. Bolstered by our maniacal hundreds, our players ascended to the top of their game. We led at the quarter by four points. The second quarter was highlighted by Jesse's behind-the-back pass to Jim Wirges, playing for the suspended Jimmy. The pass was almost a duplicate of the one which had convinced me months before that John Mercer knew a "gift" when he saw one. Jim made the catch as if it were the most natural thing to have a teammate zip the ball 15 feet in such an acrobatic way. His layup provoked unbounded delight from our followers, some of whom I thought were going to jump out of their shoes, so violently did they leap up from their seats.

I was surprised at how little we were missing the Alphesons, whom I saw in the stands, gleeful and grateful that the Anglers' performance would give them a chance to play in the finals. I didn't see Tradeau, although I spent no time hunting for him. I mainly watched the scoreboard as it showed that time was decreasing and our lead was increasing. We won by 14 points, and I really didn't care what "Mad" Donner had to say about Jewelton in the next day's paper—we had made it to the finals!

CHAPTER TWENTY-TWO

The Jewelton Anglers were to play the Jericho Demons for the class B state basketball championship on Saturday, March 11, 1961. Those were the facts of the matter—on the surface. To thousands of people in our state, and millions, even billions of people elsewhere, it was a matter that was of no consequence, because it wasn't known to exist. But to those who were caught up in the event, it had become the most important thing in the world. Politics, the movement of armies, natural disasters, scientific breakthroughs—all of life's really significant events and issues took a back seat to 32 minutes of a game played by students in high school. I realized late Friday night that the contest had become much more than a game.

Civic pride was involved: "Our town is better than your town because we beat you." It was a matter of ego: "I defeated you; therefore I'm better than you." These considerations were part of the game, whether one wanted to admit them or not. Players' parents and close friends were swept up into a frenzy of hope—the hope that the young men they were identified with would validate their own worth by prevailing in the game. The desire to be proclaimed the best was so compelling that thousands of people felt that their personal happiness, if only its temporary state, depended on the efforts of teenagers.

The adulation that our team received after beating Horizon was responsible for evoking my thoughts about what winning had come to mean—at least for the people of Jewelton who were there. My speculation was that for every Angler fan who was ecstatic in Jericho, 10 back in Jewelton felt the same way, or would if the Anglers won. I didn't see anything wrong in the phenomenon of adults being so enthralled by the achievements of youth. I perceived it as a natural response to the pride that they experienced when their own did well in competition. The championship game, with all the hopes and fears it generated, wasn't just a sporting event. It was a referendum at the highest level for an entire community: a vote, thumbs up or down, on a way of life. Over the years, people not intimately involved would forget the verdict, but the towns involved would never forget. It was a heavy burden for boys from 15 to 18 to carry. Every bear hug, every pat on the back, every "Way to go!" added to the weight of it, for the unspoken message was that the job, regardless of how excellently executed, was not a real success until it was a total success—that meant the winning of one more game.

I believe the pressure I acknowledged on Friday night began to be seen on Saturday morning. It may have appeared odd to an outsider, but the Anglers were not uniformly happy. They were quiet at breakfast, almost moody. Matt reported that Jude Alpheson and Tradeau got into a loud argument which almost turned into a fight. The source of the disagreement was ostensibly who used whose toothpaste, but I suspected it had to do with Friday's suspension and their opposite reactions to it. Matt also said that Tradeau had not attended the Horizon game. He bragged that he had picked up a Jericho girl and went to the movies instead.

Coach Levitson gave everyone the morning off. I was relieved that no tour or team activity was planned. I wasn't exactly down in the dumps, but I was close. Very few of the players were inclined to wander far from the hotel. They visited with family and friends or went to their rooms. Pete, Johnny, Tom, and I all made our way separately back to our room soon after breakfast. Occasional bursts of enthusiasm about the game were counterpointed by long periods of staring at each other, out the window, or at the children's Saturday morning television offerings.

Both Jewelton and Jericho had been allotted 375 tickets for the game. A prospective buyer of the prized tickets had to present a driver's license to make a purchase, with the number that he or she bought being subtracted from the total allotted to each community. If either town had not acquired its quota by seven o'clock, which was 30 minutes before game time, the leftovers would be sold indiscriminately. It was nice to know that potentially our crowd could be as large as theirs, although I doubted that our fans would buy up all the tickets available to them. In the afternoon, however, I began to see more and more people from Jewelton whom I hadn't seen the night before. They were drawn to the hotel by the knowledge that the team and its fans were staying there. Exuberant Angler backers were replacing the numbers of people the Noble had lost during the week as teams fell and went home.

The most gratifying thing that happened all that morning and afternoon was the reading and re-reading of the newspaper's story regarding our win against Horizon. "Mad" Donner had been taken off the basketball beat for at least one night, and his replacement, a Jerry Wilder, was very generous in his praise of the Anglers' efforts. I didn't care that he relied heavily on the clichés of calling us the tournament's "Cinderella" team and the "dark horse" too, even though I had been taught by Mr. Levitson, as English teacher, that, used together, they constituted a mixed metaphor, a thing to be avoided in good writing. As the afternoon ended, I concluded that my three roommates' somber mood was a combination of pressure and a realistic appraisal of our chances against Jericho. The Demons had won their three games by an average of 20 points. The name Dan Brothers echoed over and over in the talk about Jericho. Brothers was the tournament's leading scorer and rebounder—the personification of what might be called the white person's stereotype of the great black player. He was huge but moved with speed and grace. Although he was playing in the state's smallest classification, he was said to be scouted by the biggest and best-known colleges in America. Kentucky and North Carolina and UCLA may have wanted to see more of Brothers, but we weren't eager to see him at all. I couldn't help remembering Mercer's reference to a player like Brothers as what the people of Jewelton and other places imagined when they thought about the type of black player who could change the destiny of their teams. I smiled when I thought of the tremendous contrast between Brothers and Jesse. Our great black player had scored about 25 points all year. His rebound total was only slightly more. But what Jesse meant to our team was at least as much as what Brothers meant to his. Jesse had led the way to an acceptance of what Coach wanted the Anglers to do. Jesse had proved to 12 other players, three of them on the playground and nine of them in the gym, that to give up the ball was our team's cardinal virtue. If Brothers changed places with Jesse, would the Anglers be in the finals? I doubted it. We had made it this far on a wave of belief rather than talent. Our thirteen believed that if they worked hard enough for long enough, they would find a teammate who could score. That was the spirit of Jesse Crosse, and it had been that which accounted for the upset of Columbia. With Brothers on our side against Columbia, the inspiration to hold the ball resolutely would never have occurred to the Jewelton team. We would have tried to match them basket for basket, playing conventionally, and our supporting cast for Brothers could not have taken up enough slack to cope with the talented, but now departed Captains. In short, Brothers was the star of the tournament, but I wouldn't have traded Jesse for him.

　　I was happy to see a mammoth pile of lima beans on my supper dish. Their mysterious properties might work their magic once more. The tension at the long table was palpable, and I tried to relieve it by talking earnestly, though probably aimlessly, to anyone who would listen. As it turned out, nobody did. As I would get one's attention, I could see his eyes begin to glaze over after my first couple of sentences. It was hopeless trying to take their minds off the Jericho juggernaut. I suspected that the specter of Brothers had taken on such legendary proportions that our guys would have believed that professional, not college, scouts were interested in him. There was only one thing left to do: play the game.

Nunn Field House was jammed. And the people on the north side, which was nearly half the crowd, were from Jewelton. So far, we were even. The intensity and duration of the hosannas emanating from each side were the same. Still even. When Jericho took the floor, we were no longer even.

The appearance of the 6'4" Brothers wouldn't have been so depressing if he hadn't been typical of the size of Jericho's dozen players. There seemed to be a mold in Jericho from which their players sprung. Make two or three white ones, then a black one, then some more white ones, and then another black one! Were the people of Jericho especially tall? Was that why their sons were so big? Were they closer to the equator than Jewelton? I had once read that children who lived near that geographic dividing line grew faster than those farther away. But the explanation for the phenomenon wasn't as important at the moment as the fact of it. Our two tallest were Tom and Pete, and they wouldn't even be playing at the same time. Rebounds were going to be scarce.

Back in the dressing room, Coach Levitson was relaxed. He was at the very edge of his career's highest achievement, and yet he showed no tension. He had coached for more than two decades and had never gotten this close to the championship. Ice water in the veins? Coach had been very clinical in his discussion of Jericho earlier in the day, and had delivered nothing like a pep talk. It was about to come—the most moving exhortation that he could create, I presumed.

"Boys, there's only one thing wrong with getting to the finals as far as I can see. It's not very much fun. People from home come zooming into Jericho full of good wishes, but there's one thing more that they've got with them. You've seen it, I know. It's a kind of desperate look in their eyes. It is full of anxiety about the last game. 'Can you do it for us one more time?' that look seems to say. You have noticed it, haven't you?"

The nods all around the room were accompanied by smiles. The players were no strangers to "the look." Coach waited to see if he was finding agreement, then he said, "Boys, maybe the first three games were, in a way, for the folks back home. They derived a great deal of pride from those victories.

We didn't exactly put Jewelton on the map with those wins, but we got people all over the state to know where we are on the map. That's fine. I'm glad we've given our people so much pleasure by going this far. But tonight's game is not for them. And it's not for me. I may make it back to the state tournament again. I know I haven't been here very often, but the opportunity is there for me, every year. The same thing is true for our fans. If we come back again next year or in five years, they'll have the experience all over again. But it is certain that our five seniors will never be back. It's not likely that we could do this again for the next two years in a row either. It's possible, but not likely. So this is, for some, the absolute last chance to play in the finals. For others, it's a long shot that you'll ever get another chance. So tonight's game is for you. This is your reward for your fine efforts this year. A reward shouldn't make you tense or anxious. It should make you happy, which is not exactly the way I'd describe you've been acting today." We had to laugh, thinking of the tension-filled day. It had been anything but happy.

"If it's possible for you, try to see that the honor of making it this far should bring you joy in your accomplishment. We haven't had the athletes that any of our opponents have had. We don't have them tonight. A man would be a fool to try to convince himself otherwise. But we have beaten those better teams. I don't see any reason why we won't beat Jericho tonight. So what if they're bigger? Better? It hasn't mattered before; why should tonight be any different? If you can get out from under all the responsibility for doing something for the fans and friends and realize that worrying about them is only going to detract from the pleasure of playing for the championship, I believe that we will win again. I ask you to remember that this is a game. If we play it as one, I think we will have an advantage over Jericho, whose players in the warm-up looked like they were preparing to be led to the electric chair."

The widespread laughter that comment evoked meant that all of us had noticed the grim visages of the Demon players. I was certainly relaxing because of what Coach was saying, and the players looked a lot calmer too. Coach's final comment dissipated the remaining tension and got the team raring to play: "I thought I might mention too, that your teammate who has had the prophetic dreams has confided to me that although he got no details in his sleep last night about the game itself, he does have a clear memory of you players throwing me into the showers. I can conclude only one thing about that in reference to tonight's game. So, go have some fun!"

The Anglers who took to the floor were a happy bunch. They were grinning and pummeling each other playfully as we huddled, and the spirit of playing a game was upon them. The White unit looked almost frivolous in comparison to their somber opponents as they cheerfully shook hands all around. The referee tossed the ball, and the game was on.

The first shot by Brothers was a 20-foot swisher that delighted the Demons' adherents. He then blocked what I thought was a sure basket by Tom. The scouts from Kentucky and North Carolina and UCLA may have been licking their chops, but Brothers had us licking our wounds. The guy was phenomenal! Watching him for two minutes convinced me of that. Our guys were not playing scared, however, and Tom sank a shot similar to that which Brothers had earlier rejected, making the score 4-2 for Jericho.

The Whites played hard, but the Demon lead extended to 16-10 by the end of the first quarter. I was optimistic, though. I thought the Reds, with Jesse, were a better unit and could close the gap. They did. Jesse was showing no ill effects of his hospitalization and recovery, even though he was playing in his fourth game in four days. He was, in his own way, as dominant for Jewelton as Brothers was for Jericho. Jesse made four steals in the quarter, thereby depriving the Demons of a possible eight points. The Anglers also scored on three of those occasions. The fans on both sides found plenty to cheer about as the shooting was great from both teams. We also scored four times on fast breaks led by Jesse, and the score at the half was tied at 33.

Coach was unstinting in his praise. He had little more to say than that he was positive we were confounding the experts who presumed we'd be out of the game by halftime. "Boys, I imagine that over in the Jericho locker room they're trying to comprehend why they can't beat you. They just might be getting the feeling that I've got—that we are the team that is meant to win this tournament, no matter how good the opposition."

The Demons got back their six-point lead in the third quarter—and then some. It was 50-41 at the final turn. Tom, who had the job of trying to stay with Brothers, was absolutely exhausted at the end of the quarter. Brothers looked as strong as ever, and I hoped that Pete could slow him down in the last period. Brothers was murdering us! He made 14 points in the quarter just finished, and another outburst like that would cook our collective goose.

We scored first, when Jesse made yet another steal and fed Johnny for the two points. Pete electrified us all when he blocked Brothers' shot, grabbed the ball, and dribbled the length of the court for another basket. We were down by only five. We went even crazier when one of Jericho's guards, trying too hard to get the ball to Brothers, threw it out of bounds. Jesse's bullet-pass to Pete for a layup cut the margin to three. It was like the Columbia game all over again as the Anglers rebounded a miss and passed and passed the ball, relentlessly looking for the basket to bring them within a point. It was so loud in the field house that in a way it seemed like there was no sound at all. The boom was nearly sonic. The referee's whistle was almost impossible to hear. When a Demon tipped the ball out of bounds, the referees had to wave their hands to indicate to the scorer to stop the clock. When the ball came back in play, Bart Holeman finally dared a shot. Although I couldn't hear myself above the hysterical hubbub, I know I laughed at the sight of him gleefully bounding back down court when the ball found its mark. The other Anglers were also ecstatic after Bart's shot. Even though they were still ahead, Jericho's players weren't having nearly as much fun as we were.

There were five minutes left, and Jericho's lead had all but disappeared. It was 61-60. The Demons really needed to score to regain the momentum. I knew, as did everyone else, that it would be Brothers. Pete, who was doing his utmost to stay with him, knew it would be Brothers, too. It was fascinating to realize that of the 10 bodies on the court, one need only concentrate on two in order to see the crucial play. Brothers had the ball. He faked a shot, and Pete fell for it. Brothers went for the goal, which was unprotected. Pete recovered and took off after him. Brothers went high for the layup, but Pete fouled him. Brothers would have to shoot free throws to make the two points. Both players fell heavily to the floor. The mid-air collision had unbalanced them both, and they landed hard. Pete's foul wasn't a vicious one, just a determined effort to insure that the shot didn't go in. Even though the Jericho fans booed vehemently, neither official acted as if there were anything extraordinary about the contact. But Brothers did not get up!

Jericho's best lay on the shiny hardwood, writhing. He was obviously hurt. Being tempted by that in me which is evil and small and self-serving, I began to contemplate what would be the outcome if Brothers could play no more. Jericho relied on him so heavily that it would knock the life out of the team. I suddenly realized what a reproachful thing I was about to wish for—that a great player would be injured so that we could win. I further acknowledged that the hypothesis I was entertaining amounted to the desire to beat Jericho at less than its best. I didn't like what I discovered about myself at that moment. Coach Levitson came over to me and told me to take our first aid kit to the area where Brothers was lying. He said we might have something in it that could prove helpful. "Don't butt in; just be there if they need you."

When I got near the group around Brothers, I could see that he was grimacing and clutching his right hand. His shooting hand! The malignant ideas were making their way into my mind again. I banished them by listening to the conversation taking place. One of the people kneeling over Brothers was apparently a doctor. I heard him say to the panicked Jericho coach: "The thumb looks broken to me. I can't tell without an X-ray, of course. He's through."

When I looked at the pained expression of Brothers and his coach, I detested my earliest thoughts about his injury. Standing near the fallen Demon were Jesse and Pete. Pete was grief stricken at what had happened and was muttering over and over, "I wasn't trying to hurt him." Jesse, hands on hips, was intently looking at the doctor. Then he stepped up to where the coach and doctor were kneeling and knelt himself. I assumed he was going to apologize to Brothers. Instead, he reached out for the injured hand, and before the doctor could finish saying, "What the hell are you doing?" he pulled on the injured thumb. Brothers gave a startled groan and a questioning look at Jesse. Jericho's coach grabbed Jesse's jersey and said, "Have you gone crazy?" Jesse replied softly, "I think he's OK now."

Brothers was gingerly flexing his hand, and then he did it vigorously. "Hey, coach, he's right! It feels fine!" Brothers proclaimed. The doctor and coach exchanged astonished looks. "Are you sure?" the doctor asked. "Yeah, it's OK, just like he said."

Both men turned to Jesse for an explanation. He offered none. He stood up and rejoined Pete, who was astounded too by what had taken place. The fans couldn't have seen any of the details of what Jesse had done. Brothers was back on his feet and was cheered by Jericho and Jewelton fans alike. When Brothers went to the foul line, the cheers from the Jericho fans reached a crescendo, as they no doubt were enormously relieved that their bellwether had not been put out of action. None of us close to Jesse's action could explain it. The only available fact was that Brothers appeared lost, but through Jesse's intervention, was renewed. Play resumed and Brothers made both his shots. Jericho was ahead by three, 63-60.

The intensity of the last five minutes was almost unbearable. The players outdid all they had done before. The manic crowd witnessed great shots, hard-fought rebounds, and pinpoint passes. Thirty seconds remained and Jericho led by one point, 69-68. What was worse, the Demons had the ball. There was no reason for them to shoot again. The one-point lead would be plenty. Their guards were doing an excellent job of eluding the various traps which Coach had taught our players for just such an occasion. I knew that if they followed his directions, they would foul somewhere between the 15- and 10-second mark. They would foul the player they thought was least likely to make his free throws.

The trouble was that all of Jericho's shooters were good, so the choice didn't matter very much. The clock hit 00:15, and I began to anticipate the waving hands of the officials, who signaled through the din that a foul had taken place. But the seconds oozed by and no foul was called! Were our players going to let them run out the clock? Had they forgotten Coach's instructions? He had even reminded them of what to do at our last timeout.

I leaped out of my seat when Pete ripped the ball from the hands of the man Andy was guarding. Pete had taken the awful gamble that he could leave Brothers and sneak up unseen. It worked! Jesse snatched the ball and called timeout—our last. We would in-bound the ball at the free-throw line, about 75 feet from our goal. Seven seconds remained.

Huddling nervously, everyone looked to Coach for one last play. He was in no hurry to give them the details. As the crowd sent waves of sound across Nunn Field House, he was walking back and forth, conjuring up our last try, I supposed. He finally came to the circle of expectant players and said, "You guys remember the first game with Apollo?"

The players dipped their heads up and down to indicate they did, but that didn't mean they understood what he was driving at. "I want to run that play again." What play? What did he mean? "Bart and Pete, I hope you don't mind being taken out at this point, but I want Phil and Tom to do what they did on that play again."

He began to describe the assignments and I began to recollect "that play." Jesse would probably be guarded tightly on the in-bounds pass, and Phil would throw it instead to Tom, who would run to the ball from our line of four men facing Phil. The idea was to have Jesse, benefiting from screens by his teammates, break for the goal and get the long pass from Tom. But surely Jericho wouldn't leave their goal unguarded. They'd never fall for it! Coach told Phil and Tom to check in. We had one last chance to win.

The first part of the play worked to perfection. The Demons were guarding each of the Anglers closely, trying to make it tough to get the ball down court in seven seconds. Jesse was given a long look by Phil, who then acted as if he gave up on Jesse, who was by then peeling off two screens and headed down court. Phil turned his attention to Tom. Tom came to meet Phil's pass and wheeled to our basket to find Jesse, who had streaked for the goal. But Jericho was too smart. Unscreened and standing tall between Jesse and the goal was Dan Brothers. He would intercept a long, cross-court pass to Jesse, who had broken free of his man. But Jesse saw that Brothers would capture a long pass. So he stopped and waved his arm to Tom, beckoning him to fire the ball right then and there. Tom realized it was our only chance, so he let it fly. Jesse caught the ball in the open, but he was 30 feet from the goal. Five seconds to go.

Brothers moved quickly into the lane to challenge Jesse if he tried to drive to the goal. Jesse had to drive anyway and try to draw a foul. Brothers was almost a foot taller, and he would surely block any shot near the goal, but maybe he would foul in the process. Three seconds.

Jesse sized up his options and then made his choice. He dribbled once and then stopped—and shot. It was the kind of shot that he had told Coach he didn't take—the one-handed long rainbow that was typical of so many other guards, but one that he had passed up at the try-out and had never before taken in a game. Pete wouldn't be under the goal to grab a lofted pass this time. One second!

And then we were state champions. The shot, actually more of a heave, rattled the rim, and I distinctly heard it, so quiet had the field house become. The Jewelton Anglers had beaten them all.

CHAPTER TWENTY-THREE

Fifty years after the winning shot, I can still see Pete running to Jesse and picking him up. Jesse hadn't moved since he shot. Pete hoisted him and circled with his teammate held high, as if making certain that everyone would get one last good look at the little hero before all the players were lost in the sea of delirious Jewelton fans cascading out of the bleachers.

Coach Levitson later got the dunking in the showers prophesied in the dream. A day or two after we got back from the tournament I asked Coach Levitson about the dreams. He confirmed my suspicion that the visions had been Jesse's. I wondered if there wasn't something almost supernatural about the ability to see the future in dreams. Fascinated for years by this phenomenon, I've read several books on the subject. The authors' unanimous agreement is that a miniscule number of people have shown uncanny ability to see future events in their sleep. Every writer pointed out that no one demonstrating this power has ever been 100% correct in his or her predictions. I couldn't be sure, but as far as I knew, Jesse never missed on one of his.

In those days after the final victory, I kept trying to figure out what Jesse had done to Brothers' hand. There was some comment after the game about Jesse's assist of Brothers, but the people talking about it were discussing it as something less than what I thought it was. Their view was the Jesse had been very sportsmanlike to manipulate the thumb of Brothers until it popped back into its proper position. I talked to Pete about it, since he had witnessed it too, and he was also convinced that the injury seemed like a whole lot more than just a thumb out of joint. "But I guess that's what it must have been, don't you, Doc? That doctor who thought it was broken must have just been all shook up and thought it was worse than it was. Heck, I don't know what Jesse did. Maybe he healed him on the spot!" Pete's laughter indicated that he knew he was talking absurdly, but it only made me wonder if he wasn't saying something that both of us recognized was impossible, yet something that we both suspected might have taken place nevertheless.

Jewelton was a crazy place for two weeks after we won the tournament. When our bus arrived from Jericho on Sunday just before noon, we saw a banner draped from one side to the other of Dolor Street. It proclaimed the championship, welcomed the players back, and trumpeted the town's pride. What looked to me like more people than lived in Jewelton lined the street and waved and yelled at us as we drove by. Monday was declared a free day by Mr. Abrams. A banquet was scheduled for the following Friday for Coach Levitson to present the championship trophy to the school board's president. Players later reported that they were cornered everywhere they went, urged to discuss the events of the week in Jericho. Johnny told me one day, "I wouldn't have believed I'd ever say this, but I'm starting to get sick of talking about the tournament. They want to know everything! 'What did you eat that night for supper? How long did you sleep that afternoon?' The only thing I haven't been asked is how often I went to the bathroom, and I wouldn't be surprised if that came up eventually."

The exhilaration did finally begin to taper off, though an announcement was made at school that a collection taken at the local businessmen's meeting would pay for a sign to be erected at the city limits. It would inform all who entered Jewelton that the Anglers were the 1961 champions. Other than that, life was getting back to normal. We had only the last quarter of the school year left. We seniors were talking about our futures, summer or permanent jobs, and we were just trying to survive until graduation.

On Monday, April 8, school was dismissed at 2:30 so that students could go to the gym for the unveiling of the sign informing all who drove into the western outskirts of Jewelton that we were the champs. Apparently there wasn't enough money to pay for another marker at the east side of town, but we were impressed enough by the one not to gripe about the other's nonexistence. I wasn't too thrilled about the inclusion of a fishing rod painted next to the word Anglers, but other than that, the sign brought back our fondest memories, and that made it a nice addition to the Jewelton scene.

Johnny came over to my house that night to study for an English test. Mr. Levitson was not cooperating at all with the seniors' desires. We wanted to just slide on through the remainder of the school year with as little friction as possible. He was bound and determined that we were going to study tons of material relating to 20th century British Literature. Johnny and I were quizzing each other about people named Sitwell and Orwell when my mother appeared at my bedroom door with a worried look on her face. "There's someone here to see you," she curtly said. She stepped back from the door and allowed Tradeau to pass into the room. He was unmistakably drunk. He stumbled in, reeking of beer, and was almost hysterical.

"You've got to do something to help me!" he babbled. "Something very bad may be happening and we've got to stop it!" Johnny and I had no idea what he was talking about, or why he had come to my house looking for help. If there was one player among the Anglers who didn't end the season on a happy note, it was Tradeau. His suspension for the game with Horizon was followed by only a short stint playing against Jericho. He was clearly unhappy with Coach Levitson's use, or misuse as he saw it, of him. His disposition had soured following the tournament, and he had disassociated himself from the other team members. So why had he come to see me?

Tradeau slumped in my chair and said nothing. He was alternating between periods of agitation and near-sleep. When I asked him what was wrong, it was as if my question suddenly reminded him of his mission. He leaned forward abruptly and said, almost crying, "Two guys have got Crosse. I don't even know who they are. They said they just wanted to scare him, but now I'm not so sure."

He began to fall back in his chair again, but Johnny leaped off the bed, grabbed his shirt, shook him, and demanded, "What are you talking about? What's happened to Jesse?"

Tradeau gave him a pitiful look and confessed, "These two guys gave me a six-pack of beer. I didn't even know them. I just ran into them down at Monroe's." Monroe's Drive-In was a local hamburger stand with lots of teen-aged customers. Tradeau rambled on, "They just said they wanted to play a little trick on him. They told me they wanted to convince him to stay away from Maggie and the other white girls. They said they wouldn't hurt him—just wanted to scare him. I didn't go along with it at first, but they kept handing me beers, and I finally said OK. They told me they'd give me a case of beer if I'd call Crosse and tell him I was in trouble and needed to talk to him. They had me tell him not to talk to anybody about where he was going, or why. You know what a sucker Crosse is for anybody in trouble. I called him; he said he'd come, and I told him to meet me in the little parking lot behind the gym; you know, where Levitson parks."

Tradeau almost nodded off again, and that time I grabbed him by the collar and shook him awake. He managed to continue. "These two guys gave me my beer—even put it in the trunk of my car for me. Just like they said they would. They thanked me and took off. I started wondering what they'd do, so I thought I'd drive by school to see what was up. I parked out in front of the gym and walked around back. When I got there…oh God, I didn't think they were going to hurt him!"

Tradeau held his head with both hands, as if to keep out memories, and I was afraid he was going to pass out before he finished his story. I slapped him hard, and he came up cursing. "Wake up, Tradeau! What did you see?"

Despite the slap, his eyes rolled back in his head, and he passed out. I shook him again but he didn't regain consciousness. What he told us was enough to make us afraid for Jesse. Our first thought was to find him. It didn't occur to us to try to enlist help. All we could think of was to get to that parking lot. I informed my mother that Tradeau was passed out on the bed, and that Johnny and I had to go out. She didn't request an explanation. She knew that something abnormal was going on but didn't make me explain. I was grateful for that.

What was happening to Jesse? That was our compelling concern—that and how fast we could get to that little-used lot.

Johnny was ordinarily an excellent driver, but he hit several curbs making turns and broke the speed limit the entire way getting to school. When we roared around the corner to the lot, our headlights showed it was empty. We stopped and ran around the wooded area next to the lot to see if Jesse were there. No sign of him. Maybe he had gotten pushed around and then had gone home. Should we call his home? We didn't. Instead we drove all over town looking for a car with Jesse in it. We drove for more than an hour. It was only then that we decided we should get help. It was perhaps natural that when we got to the telephone at the nearby Monroe's that I called Coach Levitson. I was accustomed to thinking of him as a solver of problems. I related Tradeau's tale as fast as I could. When Coach asked me how long it had been since Tradeau told us his story, I told him it was maybe 90 minutes. He sounded shocked, and so I explained that we had gone to the lot ourselves to investigate and hunted for Jesse thereafter. His pause after I said that made me think that we had done the wrong thing by not getting help from the start, but he didn't say that we had made a mistake. He said that he'd call the police.

I didn't think to ask Coach what he thought Johnny and I could do to help, so we decided to keep driving, keep looking. But it was impossible. What were we looking for? What kind of car? Old men? Young men? The total absence of information beyond Tradeau's sketchy story made our search futile. Again we drove for more than an hour and then decided to call Coach again. Maybe Jesse had turned up. Mrs. Levitson answered and told me that her husband had gone to Mrs. Crosse's house. Mrs. Levitson knew that Jesse had not been found as recently as 30 minutes before, and that the police were conducting an all-out search.

Her news chilled me. Would the men have been easier to catch if we'd called for help earlier? The question wouldn't go away, and I couldn't answer it. We drove some more. Then I thought to call home, to give my parents an idea of where I was, and what I was up to. Mom told me that Tradeau had awakened and left the house despite her urgings that he should not leave. She had already called his parents, but they didn't get there until after he had gone. "Luke, I tried to hold him by the arm, but he pulled away from me. Since your father wasn't here, there was no way I could make him stay. He was in no condition to drive, I'll tell you that." I assured Mom that she had done all that anyone could have asked of her. "I just hope that boy doesn't kill somebody driving drunk," she concluded. I briefly filled her in about Jesse and then told her we were going to continue to look for him.

But Johnny and I were getting nowhere by driving aimlessly. We decided to go to the police station to see if anything more was known about the disappearance. We also hoped that we might be able to help in some way. A sergeant named Bowers was the only one there. He was cool to our inquiries at the outset, but he was more forthcoming when we told him that we had been the ones who heard Tradeau's story. He told us that all the police on the force were conducting the search, but there was no trace of Jesse.

We stood helplessly in the police station. Sgt. Bowers had no suggestions as to how we could assist the police, other than to do what we had been doing. We were about to leave when the telephone rang. Answering it, the sergeant repeated and wrote down what that the caller told him: About five miles west of town, in a big field across the highway from an auto salvage dealer, a cross had been seen burning. The trademark of the Klan! Johnny and I didn't hang around to listen to more. We did hear Bowers yelling at us though. He was ordering us not to go to the scene of the cross burning. "There could be trouble." There was.

In less than 10 minutes, Johnny and I got to the general area which had been reported as the scene of the burning cross. Officer Smith had been in the car that we trailed there, and we pulled up behind him. There was no cross burning. Maybe the report was a hoax—another version of a snipe hunt. Smith had drawn his pistol. He wasn't happy to see us. "How did you boys know to come here? Were you following me?"

Johnny assured him that we hadn't been knowingly trailing him, but that we had overheard the call at the police station. The darkness enveloped us. No moon or star cast any light. If the burning cross had burned out, it wouldn't be easy to find. Reluctantly, Smith enlisted our aid. We walked into a field made soggy by a morning thunderstorm. We walked about 15 feet apart and followed the weak beam of Smith's flashlight as he played it back and forth on the ground in front of us. We combed the field. Nothing. I was convinced that there was no cross, but Smith was determined to cover every inch of the field before leaving. It was slow, time-consuming work.

The field ended in some woods, and we walked the length of the open area from the road and back to the woods several times. The mud on our shoes was thick and getting thicker. Johnny and I were laboring to keep up with Smith. I began to think that Smith might do better to get back on the road if he wanted to find Jesse.

"What's that?" Johnny shrieked. Smith and I turned in Johnny's direction. He was pointing to a portion of the field that abutted the woods. Smith aimed his flashlight in that direction. The cross was there; actually we could see two crosses. In a harsh voice that was not to be disobeyed, Smith told us to stay back. We did. He approached one cross. The light was faint, but it was enough to show Smith in silhouette. The policeman who had worked so hard to find out who had beaten Jesse emitted an agonized moan and went down on one knee. "Oh, no!" escaped from his lips as if he were a man being tortured. Jesse was hanging from a cross. The burned cross stood next to it.

CHAPTER TWENTY-FOUR

What went through the minds of the men who killed Jesse Crosse? Had they actually planned to murder him or were they intent on terrifying him, as they had told Tradeau? A summary of the coroner's report was published in the paper. It revealed that Jesse had been beaten and whipped. He was alive when they lifted him to the cross and tied him to it with ordinary clothesline. The coroner found that Jesse had died of suffocation, after hanging for about three hours. In his weakened condition from the beating, the weight of his body, slight though he was, simply overwhelmed the power of his lungs to continue to supply him with air. The agony and terror of that slow death horrifies the imagination. Whether his killers knew or thought he would die has never been discovered because they were never found.

It is 50 years since I was one of the three to find Jesse in that field. It has only been in the last year or two that I have been able to think very long about that discovery. Although I have become a doctor and have dealt with many situations which repulse the mind, none has ever been so emotionally wrenching as helping Officer Smith and Johnny take Jesse down from that cross. I was 18 then, and the combination of rage and revulsion has, fortunately, never been duplicated in my life. Somehow, Johnny and I were able, however mindlessly, to follow Smith's instructions. Although he was not much older than we were, Smith was capable of drawing on his sense of duty to direct us to do what had to be done. I hadn't been near death before, and I was horrified by what had happened to Jesse. Even though it seemed certain that Jesse was dead when we found him, Smith valiantly tried mouth-to-mouth resuscitation for several minutes. He told Johnny to go back to the patrol car. Smith carefully instructed him as to how he could call the police station on the radio. He told Johnny to order an ambulance.

When Johnny returned, he said that Sgt. Bowers had informed him that the town's only ambulance was out on a call and wouldn't get to us for another half hour. Smith kept up his doomed attempt to revive Jesse for a few more minutes. He then sat in the mud, exhausted. I asked him if I should try to revive Jesse. "No, he's gone."

The night that was a nightmare come to life didn't end there. When the ambulance arrived, the driver and his assistant reported to Smith that they were delayed because of a call to the scene of a one-car wreck. They said that the driver had been killed. Smith asked who had died. "A kid named Tradeau." was the answer.

Johnny and I followed the ambulance as it wended its way slowly back to town, following Officer Smith's car. We followed the ambulance to the hospital without giving thought as to why. Coach Levitson and Mrs. Crosse were standing outside the emergency entrance, waiting for what they had been told was coming. Oh, the sorrow of a mother! Surely Mrs. Crosse was devastated, but somehow she was not destroyed. She asked to see Jesse. Officer Smith signaled the hesitant ambulance attendant to pull back the sheet which covered Jesse's face. It would be the first time I had viewed him in the light, and my stomach turned over at the thought of it, but I had to see him again.

It was incredible that his face was unmarked. In death, he was as peaceful as if he were only asleep. Mrs. Crosse didn't break down. She kissed Jesse and softly said, "Now you're with your father." She stepped away, and the ambulance crew took Jesse into the hospital. Mrs. Crosse went in with him, and was met at the door by Mrs. Levitson, Mrs. Abrams, and some other women. Coach stayed outside at the emergency entrance with Johnny, Officer Smith, and me. I was feeling very sharply the pangs of guilt for having failed to get help right away, but I couldn't bear to mention what might have been our colossal mistake. Coach Levitson's intuition was infallible. "Luke and Johnny, you did your best tonight. Don't ever forget that or doubt that." I have doubted it, many times, but I haven't forgotten, and I've always been grateful for the Coach's words. Even though our decisions might not have been the correct ones, I have come to believe what Coach said to us that night.

Tradeau's death was not a subject that I could grapple with that night. I found out the next day that he had driven his car into a brick wall at a speed of over 65 miles per hour. He had broken his neck in the collision. Officer Smith told me some months later that the policeman who had investigated the scene told him that Tradeau may have driven into the wall on purpose, that the wreck might have been suicide; no skid marks prior to impact suggested that view.

We attended two funerals that week but only one burial. J.I. Tradeau was interred in the Jewelton cemetery, but Jesse's mother took him back to their hometown, Flower, 200 miles away, to be buried next to his father. I've visited his grave twice in 50 years. The second time was earlier today, March 11, the day that his shot won the tournament. I have wondered a lot about what Jesse would have done with his life if he'd had it to live. He had just turned 16 when he died, and it's hard for me to believe that he would be 66 now. If anyone was ever destined to be a doctor or a minister, I think it was Jesse. His willingness to do for others, and his ability to take away pain or remove the threat to another's well-being was amply demonstrated in his short life. I have, to the limitations of my character, tried in many ways to emulate the doctor that I believe Jesse Crosse would have been. His influence on my life has been profound. He was someone whose life should not be forgotten.

The passing of years has certainly caused the memory of Jesse to fade in Jewelton. His murder so shocked us, those who knew him and loved him, that we have always had a hard time discussing it. As a result, we haven't talked about Jesse. But it is to our shame that we haven't kept his story alive. Recently I was bluntly reminded of my negligence in this matter. I was driving by a junior high where I presently live and saw four short kids playing basketball outside. Three were white and one was black. The little black kid nonchalantly flipped a pass behind his back. Kids of today can do that sort of thing on a basketball court with ease—a skill that was all but unknown 50 years ago. I momentarily thought that I was looking at the ghosts of Si, Bart, Phil, and Jesse, just biding their time until Mercer discovered them. I knew then that the ghosts could come back to life only if someone would make known who they were and what they had done. I had an obligation to fulfill.

It was for that reason that I made the trip to Jewelton after 50 years. At an assembly of all the students I presented a bronze plaque to Jewelton High School. Mr. Abrams, the son of our principal, who took his father's place, accepted it. The plaque was a memorial to the 1961 state champions, what I hope will be a more lasting remembrance than the fallen, battered sign at the city limits. Mr. Abrams gave me free rein to talk about the team to a student body only vaguely aware of its accomplishments. So I told the students about that great team, and I told them about Jesse Crosse.

THE END

JESSE CROSSE

A NOVEL

EXTRAS

An explanation from the author:

Jesse Crosse is a story known as an *allegory*. Chances are you have already heard the story many times, but never told this way. It's a very old story, and some think it's the most important one ever told. If the re-telling in this allegory entertains you, or instructs you, or inspires you, that's good. It means you as reader, and I as author, have used our time well. If you will read further, you will better understand what an allegory is.

Animal Farm, as you probably know, is a novel by George Orwell, an Englishman. Here's what's odd about the novel: It has been read and enjoyed by both very young readers and readers who aren't so young (something that *Jesse Crosse* may also do). Orwell's world includes animals that not only think like people, they also talk like them. It isn't unusual for youthful readers to find such stories fascinating, as the idea of talking animals seems quite natural to them at that age. For years they have seen such characters in movies, television, and books and are accustomed to their skills in speech.

It's surprising to hear how adults have read with great interest a book featuring animals that have conversations. But older readers, millions of them, have read and enjoyed *Animal Farm.* What explains the ability of *Animal Farm* to fascinate readers of all ages?

Animal Farm has the power to attract a wide-ranging audience because, as an allegory, it's a story that works on two levels: the first that can be comprehended by children and the second that older, more experienced readers can appreciate. That's what makes it an allegory. An allegory tells not only the story that any reader can understand, but also a second story: a parallel, or similar, story that a more mature reader will recognize.

Would an adult reader think that *Animal Farm* is simply a tale about animals overthrowing their human farmer and running the farm by themselves? Probably not. Such a reader will begin to see that the animals' story has a parallel in history: It's about the Russian Revolution of the early 20th century, and the animal characters in the novel have real-life counterparts in history. The pigs are like, or parallel to, the members of the Communist party, with certain pigs being like specific Communist leaders, such as Joseph Stalin and Leon Trotsky.

Why would an author use an allegory to tell a story that already exists? For one thing, it offers the possibility of interesting readers in a tale they may already know, but that they find enjoyable or instructive for being told in a new way. For another, readers can find it stimulating to see how the allegorical details develop—as if they were watching a puzzle beginning to reveal itself. Solving a puzzle is very satisfying. Why? Because one has given real thought to the details.

So *Jesse Crosse* exists on two levels. One is Luke Anteock's 50-year-old story about an extraordinary boy who deeply touched the lives of those whom he met. The other is about another young man, of 20 centuries ago, who did the same. If you give some thought to the story, you may begin to see that Jesse, and Coach Mo Levitson, and Paul Lightman, and Tom Dubius, and many more of the characters you meet in *Jesse Crosse* are familiar to you, and that their story is worth telling and reading again.

Who's Who? Identifying the parallels:

Sometimes in an allegory, the characters' names are hard to figure out.
You might find the puzzle a bit easier with a hint or two:

- The water on which Jesus walked was known by the Romans as
  the Sea of Tiberias.
- Paul Lightman gets his last name from the translation of *Lucifer*.
- Pete and Andy Barjon got the *bar* part of their last name from the
  Aramaic language. It meant *son*. The rest of the last name is their
  father's.
- Johnny and Jim Wirges' last name comes from a nickname given
  by Jesus (in the Aramaic language he mainly spoke) that meant
  "sons of thunder."
- Phil Lipscomb's, Bart Holeman's, and Si Montler's names are
  partial combinations of the originals.
- Matt Tachsman gets his last name from the occupation of the
  Matthew on whom he is based.
- Jim and Jude Alpheson got their names from the father of those
  disciples.
- Tom Dubius' last name is from an adjective often used to describe
  the original Thomas.
- J.I. Tradeau's name is a combination of an infamous man's initials
  and the Latin verb *trado*. It's a stretch!
- Jewelton is so named for the religious and ethnic group to which
  Jesus belonged.
- Flower, where Jesse lived before Jewelton, is one of the translations
  for the Hebrew noun giving Jesus' boyhood hometown its name.
- Coach Mo Levitson: details about a famous Old Testament leader
  will reveal the source of his name.
- John Mercer gets his name from the verb that means "to sink or
  lower into water," as John the Baptist did.
- Maggie is named for a woman who was a devoted follower of
  Jesus and witnessed the crucifixion.
- And Luke, the novel's narrator, gets his last name from the fact
  that the gospel writer was from Antioch.
- Last, the Old Testament book of *Isaiah* predicts that the Messiah
  will come from "the root of Jesse"—that Jesse will be the Savior's
  ancestor.

What Do You Think? Questions for discussion:

1. Is it either offensive or proper to re-tell the story of Jesus in a novel about a basketball player? Offer reasons to support your view.

2. Despite what might be called "miraculous" things he accomplished, did Jesse Crosse seem like a real person? Can you point to parts of the story that led you to your opinion?

3. Is J.I. Tradeau to be pitied or despised? What did he do or say (or both) that causes you to reach that judgment about him?

4. Before you had read the story's conclusion, did you figure out or know that Jesse was going to die? Did that have a positive or negative effect on your view of the novel? Can you explain why your opinion was affected?

5. Did you enjoy or dislike the allegorical aspect of the novel? Can you refer to specifics that led to your view?

6. Of all Jesse's teammates, the author wanted you to like Pete Barjon the most. If you did, can you explain why? If not, where did the author fail?

7. How would you describe Luke Anteock, the narrator? Was he likable? Annoying? A know-it-all? A good guy? Specifics, please, to support your interpretation.

8. With which character did you identify most? What qualities do the two of you share? What actions did the character take that you admired. That you disliked?

Who Said It? (And why was it important to the story?):

1. "Coach, we've had enough. You win. Everything."
2. "Coach, we don't shoot from that far out."
3. "These two guys gave me a six-pack of beer."
4. "It's jammed!"
5. "Hey, Coach, he's right! It feels fine!"
6. "Anteock, my boy, you will have to see for yourself what I have found."
7. "Mr. Abrams gave me free rein to talk about the team ..."
8. "Well, I just hope that boy doesn't kill somebody driving drunk."
9. "Then the door opened. And I saw someone swim away from it."
10. "Coach, people don't talk about the Klan around here. That doesn't mean it doesn't exist."

Biographical sketch:

Mike Moran was born in St. Louis. He lived for the first eight years in Kirkwood, a St. Louis suburb. His dream as a boy was to play third base for the Cardinals, but after moving to Little Rock, that baseball dream gave way to basketball. He played as a Holy Souls Wabbit in grade school and then a Rocket at Catholic High. He has loved the game ever since, finding much truth in the words of Walt Frazier, the great ex-New York Knick: "Basketball is like poetry. You never know what's coming next."

Speaking of poetry, Mike taught that and a good deal more in 40 years as a teacher at his high school alma mater. His son John, like his father, is a C.H.S. alumnus, but unlike his father, John was class valedictorian. Mike married Cathy Wortsmith, the girl with whom he went to the Catholic High prom and who was Catholic High's homecoming queen when they were seniors—in 1961.

Mike is retired from teaching, and since retiring he wrote *Proudly We Speak Your Name*, a memoir of those 44 years (four as student, 40 as teacher) at Catholic High, which was published in 2009.

Questions for Mike Moran, author of *Jesse Crosse—A Novel:*

Q   When did you write *Jesse Crosse*?

A   I wrote it in 1984, and I have made changes to various parts off and on ever since. The basic story, however, hasn't changed. So, the answer is "NO!" to the implied question, "Did you write your novel about a small-town team that made it to the state basketball championship AFTER the movie *Hoosiers* came out?" *Hoosiers* was a 1986 release.

Q   This novel is about a boy leading a team to its greatest season ever. Isn't the novel another story as well?

A   It is. It's an allegory loosely based on the gospel of Luke. So it's the story of Jesus as well as the story of Jesse Crosse. In the Bible, Jesus was a descendant of Jesse, the father of King David; Jesus was referred to as "the root of Jesse," so that seemed an appropriate name for the protagonist.

Q The names of the characters also come from the gospel of Luke, or most of them seem to do so. Would you explain who some of those characters are in relation to the gospel?

A The narrator of the novel is Luke Anteock, the team manager/trainer, so there's your gospel writer (who was from Antioch). The team is the Jewelton Anglers, based on the fact that Jesus and the rest of his disciples were Jews—and that the disciples were, for the most part, fishermen.

Jesse has 12 teammates, which is the number of Jesus' disciples. All the players' names are variations, sometimes strained variations, on the disciples' names. Some are pretty straightforward: Matt Tachsman and Tom Dubius, for example.

Others, as I said, are a reach: characters known as Johnny and Jimmy Wirges, who are brothers, got their surname from the fact that Jesus called the disciples John and James "sons of thunder," which in Aramaic, one of the languages that Jesus used, was Boanerges. I taught several fine boys whose surname was Wirges, and I liked using that name for two of the players.

Q It will be interesting for readers to figure out where you got the names of places and people, so you are not being asked to explain them all. One name, however, seems perfectly clear and yet not clear at all. J.I. Tradeau is obviously Judas Iscariot. Will you explain Tradeau?

A To leave some pleasure for self-discovery, I say only that trado is a Latin verb in the first-person singular of the present tense. Translate that and you will understand Tradeau.

Q What thought process led to writing an allegory in which Jesse Crosse became the allegorical equivalent to Jesus Christ?

A I taught mostly English and Religion during my 40-year career at Catholic High School for Boys in Little Rock, Arkansas. One issue that I always brought up in Religion class was the Christian belief that Jesus was both God and man.

Students rather easily grasped the God part of that equation; after all, the miracles He performed and His Resurrection aren't the actions of a mere human. The belief that Jesus was a man was harder for them to consider. Sometimes I thought that my students were almost uncomfortable with my asking, "Do you think Jesus got hungry?" "Did he sweat? If so, did he bathe because he needed to?" I got the impression that delving further into his humanity was not what my hearers wanted. The idea that Jesus was really a man may have been so strange, so foreign to them that it was actually disturbing.

I concluded from their response that if Christians could identify more strongly with the man Jesus, then His generosity, His concern, His loving awareness of others' needs might not seem so difficult to imitate for us ordinary people.

And that's how Jesse came into existence. I wanted to write a novel that humanized the qualities of Jesus—a story that would give readers of all ages a figure with whom they could identify. Jesse has physical flaws (short—skinny); he's an outsider (new to Jeweleton—black); he's not what people were expecting (first black player but rarely scores a point). Despite all that, he has the power to bring people together, to break down divisions, and he's a model of the person who succeeds by giving. He sweats; he worries; he gets tired; he is injured; he befriends an outcast. Through it all, he wins, not just games but hearts as well. Though Jesse's clearly human, he exemplifies what a person, following the example of Jesus, can be.

I hope that readers of this story will find something of themselves in Jesse, either what they already are or what they want to become. If that happens, then my purpose in creating him will be achieved.

Q   Did you play high school basketball? If so, did you play the style that Jesse and his teammates played?

A   I did play, and for the same school at which I later taught for 40 years: Catholic High School for Boys. I was a substitute until my senior year. We had, in that year, a very good team, but not as good as the Jewelton Anglers. We lost in the semi-finals of the state tournament (though we beat, in the quarterfinals, in a sudden-death overtime, what many thought was the best team in the tournament—our proudest achievement).

Mr. Mike Malham and Mr. Happy Mahfouz were my two high-school coaches, the former for two years and the latter for one. They were both like Coach Mo Levitson in that they drove us hard in practice so that we were in great physical shape. When I was a senior, our team was much like Jewelton's in that we had no really tall players. Every shot had to count, and both coaches had taught us plays to run that eventually wore down the defenses, just like Jesse's team did. We weren't as fast as the Anglers, whose speed made the fast-break offense possible. We might have gotten some easy baskets like that, but not many.

Q   Is the style of basketball played by the 1961 Jewelton Anglers, with its emphasis on multiple passes and working for close-in shots, still played at any competitive level?

A   The first name that comes to mind is Princeton University, under their former coach, the legendary Pete Carril. The highly successful, controlled offense that the Tigers ran has made many converts to the style of play that depends on extraordinarily well-conditioned players running the socks off their opponents until a pinpoint pass leads to an easy two points. Many teams, both college and high school, have copied the Princeton style of play. Any player on such teams might be the high-point man for any game because all the players are able to score in this patient, good-shot-only form of TEAM basketball.

Q   Jesse Crosse is the counterpart of Jesus Christ, even to the number of letters in their names. How did you begin to develop a character in the image of the Son of God?

A   My first thought was that as the Messiah for whom the Jews had been waiting, Jesus probably disappointed or surprised many since He wasn't the military leader for whom some were hoping. Jesse was the same: the first great black basketball player in Jewelton wasn't a towering physical presence who could score at will and rebound every shot. He was a short, skinny kid who rarely scored a point. Both saviors brought a different means of salvation from the one commonly expected. That some rejected the man or boy in question isn't surprising. That they converted so many to their way is the interesting part of their stories. That's where I began with my idea of how Jesse would be portrayed.

Q   Besides Jesse, who is your favorite Angler?

A   It's the same for me as it is in the gospel: It's Peter, or in this case Pete, the rugged, never-say-die fellow who is the leader of the followers. He's not perfect, but when it comes to having a teammate to depend on, he's your guy—or at least mine.

Q   You said that you wrote this book in 1984. Have you attempted to have it published prior to 2011?

A   As I have heard other writers say, "I have a stack of rejection letters."

I did indeed try to get it published earlier. Roy Davis, my friend and colleague from Catholic High School, read my copy of Jesse many years ago, and he said to me almost annually, "Mike when are you going to get Jesse Crosse published?" My answer, like his question, was always the same: "Roy, it's not up to me. A publisher has to choose to publish it."

Q   So how, 27 years after it was first written, did *Jesse Crosse—A Novel* finally get into print?

A   The answer involves two key people: first, a long-time friend who, like Roy Davis also read the story many years ago, and who believed it should be published, and second, a publisher who came to believe the same thing. My friend Roger Armbrust, a pal for almost 60 years and who is himself a book editor, recommended the novel to Ted Parkhurst, who is the president of Parkhurst Brothers Publishing. Ted read the novel and made the decision to publish it. I told Roger, "You believed in Jesse longer than I did." Without him and Ted, Jesse Crosse would be a boy known to perhaps a dozen people.